JO NESBØ

ILLUSTRATED BY
mike LOWERY

SIMON AND SCHUSTER

First published in Great Britain in 2010 by Simon and Schuster UK Ltd
A CBS COMPANY
First published in the USA in 2010 by Aladdin, an imprint of Simon & Schuster
Children's Publishing Division
Originally published in Norway in 2007 as *Doktot Prokto's Prompepulvet*
by H. Aschehoug & Co.

Text copyright © Jo Nesbø 2007. Published by arrangement
with the Salomonsson Agency.
English translation copyright © 2010 Tara Chace
Illustrations copyright © Mike Lowery 2010

Simon & Schuster UK Ltd
1st Floor, 222 Gray's Inn Road, London WC1X 8HB

A CIP catalogue record for this book is available from the British Library.

ISBN 978-1-84738-653-3

5 7 9 10 8 6

Printed by CPI Cox & Wyman, Reading, Berkshire RG1 8EX

www.simonandschuster.co.uk

The New Neighbour

IT WAS MAY, and once the sun had shone for a while on Japan, Russia and Sweden, it came up over Oslo – the very small capital city, of a very small country called Norway. The sun got right to work shining on the yellow, and fairly small, palace that was home to the king of Norway, who didn't rule over enough for it to amount to anything, and on Akershus Fortress. There it shone on the old cannons that were aimed out over the Oslo Fjord, through the window of the Commandant's office and then onto the most remote of doors. The door that ultimately led to the city's most feared jail cell, the Dungeon of the Dead, where only the most dangerous and worst criminals were kept. The cell was empty, apart from a *Rattus norvegicus*, a little Norwegian rat that was taking its morning bath in the toilet.

The sun rose a tiny little bit higher and shone on some children in a school marching band who had practised waking up very early and putting on uniforms that itched, and who were now practising marching and playing almost in time. Because soon it would be the seventeenth of May, Norwegian Independence Day, and that was the day when all the school marching bands in the whole small country would get up very early, put on uniforms that itched and play almost in time.

And as the sun climbed a tiny little bit higher it shone on the wooden wharves on the Oslo Fjord, where a ship from Shanghai, China, had just docked. The wharf planks swayed and creaked from all the busy feet running back and forth unloading goods from the ship. Some of the sun's rays even made their way between the planks and down under the wharf to a sewer pipe that stuck out into the water.

And one single ray of sunlight made its way into the darkness of the sewer pipe making something in there gleam. Something that was white, wet and *very* sharp. Something that bore a nasty resemblance to a row of teeth. And if you knew something about reptiles, but were otherwise very stupid, you might have thought that what you were seeing were the eighteen fangs found in the jaws of the world's biggest and most feared constrictor. The anaconda. But nobody's that stupid. Because anacondas live in the jungle, in rivers like the Amazon in Brazil, not in the sewer pipes running every which way beneath the small, peaceful, northerly city called Oslo. An anaconda in the sewer? Sixteen metres of constricting muscles, a jaw the size of an inflatable swim ring and teeth like upside-down ice-cream cones? Ha, ha! Yeah, right, that would've been a sight!

And now the sun was starting to shine on a quiet street called Cannon Avenue. Some of the sun's rays shone on a red house there, where the Commandant of Akershus Fortress was eating breakfast with his wife and their daughter, Lisa. Some of the rays shone on the yellow house on the other side of the street, where Lisa's best friend used to live. But as her best friend had just moved to a town called Sarpsborg, seeing the yellow house empty made Lisa feel very lonely. Because now there wasn't anyone for Lisa to play with on Cannon Avenue. The only other kids in the neighbourhood were Truls and Trym Trane. They were the twins who lived in the big house with the three garages at the bottom of the hill, and they were two years older than Lisa. In the winter they threw rock-hard snowballs at her little red-haired head. And when she asked if they wanted to play, they pushed her down into the snow. And with icy mittens they rubbed snow into her face while christening her Greasy Lisa, Flatu-Lisa or Commandant's Debutante.

Maybe you're thinking that Lisa should've mentioned this to Truls and Trym's parents so they would rein the boys in. But that's because you don't know Truls and Trym's father, Mr Trane. Mr Trane was a fat and angry man, even fatter than Lisa's father and way, way angrier. And at least ten times as rich. And because he was so rich, Mr Trane didn't think anyone had any business coming and telling him *anything* whatsoever, and especially not how he ought to be raising his boys! The reason Mr Trane was so rich was that he had once stolen an invention from a poor inventor. The invention was a very hard, very mysterious and very secret material that was used, among other things, on prison doors to make prisons absolutely escape-proof. Mr Trane had used the money he'd made from the invention to build the big house with the three garages and to buy a Hummer. A Hummer, in case you don't know, is a big, angry car that was made to use in wars and that took up almost the whole road when Mr Trane drove up Cannon Avenue. Hummers are also awful polluters.

But Mr Trane didn't care, because he liked big, angry cars. And besides, he knew that if he crashed into someone his car was a lot bigger than theirs, so it would be too bad for them.

Luckily it would be a while until Truls and Trym could christen Lisa with snow again, because the sun had long since melted it on Cannon Avenue, and now the sun was shining on the gardens, which were green and well groomed. All, that is, except for one. The garden was scraggly, drab and unkempt, but was pleasant anyway because it had two pear trees and belonged to a small, crooked house that might possibly have been blue at one time and that was missing a fair number of roof tiles. The neighbours on Cannon Avenue rarely saw the man who lived there. Lisa had only met him a couple of times, he'd smiled and otherwise looked sort of like his garden — scraggly, drab and unkempt.

"What's that?" grumbled the Commandant as the

roar of a large engine disturbed the morning quiet. "Is that that awful Hummer of Mr Trane's?"

His wife craned her neck and peered out the kitchen window. "No. It looks like a moving van."

Lisa, who was generally a very well-behaved girl, got up from the table without having finished what was on her plate or having been excused. She ran out onto the front steps. And sure enough a moving van with the name CRAZY-QUICK written on its side was parked in front of the empty, yellow house that used to be her best friend's house. Movers were unloading cardboard boxes from the back. Lisa went down the stairs and over to the so-called apple tree in her garden by the fence to get a closer look. The men in overalls were carrying furniture, lamps and big, ugly pictures. Lisa noticed one of the movers showing the other a dented trumpet that was sitting on top of one of the cardboard boxes and then they both laughed. But she couldn't see any sign of what she'd been hoping to see – dolls, small bicycles, a pair of short skis. And that could only mean that whoever was moving in didn't have kids, at least no girls her age. Lisa sighed.

Just then she heard a voice.

"Hi!"

She looked around in surprise, but didn't see anyone.

"Hi there!"

She looked up at the tree her father said was an apple tree, but that no one had ever seen any apples on. And that now appeared to be talking.

"Not there," the voice said. "Over here."

Lisa stretched up on her tiptoes and peered down on the other side of the fence. And there was a little boy with red hair standing there. Well, not just red, actually, but bright red. And he wasn't just small, he was tiny. He had a tiny face with two tiny blue eyes and a tiny turned-up nose in between.

The only things on his face that were big, were the freckles.

"I'm Nilly," he said. "What do you have to say about that?"

He was supposed to be named William, but the priest refused to give such a tiny boy such a long name. So Billy would have to do. But the ringer of the church bells came up with a brilliant idea: a boy who was so tiny that he was *nearly* invisible should be called Nilly! His parents had just sighed and said okay, and thus the bell ringer got his way.

Lisa asked, "What do I have to say about what?"

"About my being called Nilly. It's not exactly a common name."

Lisa thought about it. "I don't know," she said.

"Good." The boy smiled. "It rhymes with 'silly', but let's just leave it at that. Deal?"

Lisa nodded.

The boy stuck his right index finger in his left ear. "And what's your name?"

"Lisa," she said.

Nilly's index finger twisted back and forth as he watched her. Finally he pulled his finger out, looked at it, gave a satisfied nod and rubbed it on his trouser leg.

"Jeez, I can't think of anything interesting that rhymes with Lisa," he said. "You're lucky."

"Are you moving into Anna's house?"

"I don't know who Anna is, but we're moving into that yellow shack over there," Nilly said, pointing over his shoulder with his thumb.

"Anna's my best friend," Lisa said. "She moved to Sarpsborg."

"Whoa, that's far," Nilly said. "Especially since she's your best friend."

"It is?" Lisa said. "Anna didn't think it was that far. She said I should just go south on the highway when I visit her."

Nilly shook his head, looking gloomy. "South is right, but the question is if the highway even goes that far. Sarpsborg is actually in the Southern Hemisphere."

"The Southern what-i-sphere?" Lisa said, shocked.

"Hemisphere," Nilly said. "That means it's on the other side of the world."

"Whoa," Lisa said, taken aback. After she thought about it a minute, she said, "Dad says that it's super warm in the south all year round, so I bet Anna can go swimming all the time now, whether it's summer or winter."

"No way," Nilly said. "Sarpsborg is so far south that it's practically at the South Pole. It's freezing. Penguins live on people's roofs down there."

"You mean it snows all year round in Sarpsborg?" Lisa asked.

Nilly nodded and Lisa shivered. Nilly pursed his lips together while at the same time pressing air out between them. It sounded like a fart. Lisa furrowed her brow, remembering how the twins had called her Flatu-Lisa. "Are you trying to tease me?" she asked. "About my nickname?"

Nilly shook his head. "Nope, I'm practising," he said. "I play the trumpet. That means I have to practise all the time. Even when I don't have my trumpet."

Lisa cocked her head to the side and looked at him. She wasn't really sure anymore if he was telling the truth.

"Lisa, you have to brush your teeth before you go to school," she heard a voice rumble. It was her dad, who'd put on his blue Commandant's uniform and was waddling towards the door with his big belly. "The ship with the gunpowder for our cannons arrived from Shanghai this morning, so I'll be home late. You be a good girl today."

"Yes, Dad," said Lisa, who was always good.

She knew it was a special day when the gunpowder arrived. It had sailed halfway around the world and had to be handled very carefully and respectfully, since it was used to fire off Akershus Fortress's Big and Almost World-Famous Royal Salute on May seventeenth, Norway's Independence Day.

"Dad," Lisa called to him. "Did you know that Sarpsborg is in the Southern . . . uh, Hemisphere?"

The Commandant stopped, looking puzzled. "Says who?"

"Nilly."

"Who's that?"

She pointed. "Nill . . ." she started, but stopped suddenly when she discovered that she was pointing at a stretch of Cannon Avenue where there was only Cannon Avenue and absolutely no sign of Nilly.

Seasick Goats

WHEN NILLY HEARD Lisa's dad tell her she had to go to school, he remembered he was supposed to go to school himself. Wherever it might be. And if he was fast maybe he would have time to eat breakfast, find his backpack and, if absolutely necessary, brush his teeth and still tag along with someone who knew the way to his new school.

He squeaked between the moving guys' legs and into the house. And there, in a cardboard box in the hallway, he saw his trumpet. He exhaled in relief, snatched it up and clutched it to his chest. Nilly and his sister and mum had arrived with the first load of stuff the night before, and the only thing he'd been worried about was whether the movers would forget the box with his trumpet in it.

He cautiously placed his lips against the mouth-piece.

"A trumpet should be kissed. Like a woman," his grandfather had always said. Nilly had never kissed a woman in his whole life, at least not like that, not right on the mouth. And truth be told he hoped he wouldn't have to either. He pressed the air into the trumpet. It bleated like a seasick goat. There aren't many people who've heard a seasick goat bleat, but that's exactly what it sounded like.

Nilly heard someone banging on the wall and knew

HONKHO
HONKHO
HONK

it was his mum, who hadn't got up yet. "Not now, Nilly!" she yelled. "It's eight a.m. We're sleeping."

She pretty much always said "we", even if she was alone in her bedroom: "We're going to bed now" and "We're going to make ourselves a cup of coffee." As if Nilly's dad weren't gone at all, as if she still had him in there – stored in a little box, and every once in a while when Nilly wasn't there, she would take him out. A tiny miniature dad who looked like the dad Nilly had seen in pictures. Miniature meant that something was really small and it made sense that of all people, Nilly would have a miniature dad, since Nilly was the smallest boy Nilly had ever seen.

He went down to the kitchen and made himself some breakfast. Even though they'd just moved in the day before, he found everything he needed, because they'd moved so many times, he pretty much knew where his mum would put stuff. The plates in the cupboard on the left, the silverware in the top drawer and the bread in the drawer below that. He was about to sink his teeth into a thick slice of bread with salami on top when it was snatched out of his hands.

"How you doing, dwarf?" Eva asked, sinking her teeth exactly where Nilly had been planning to sink his teeth. Eva was Nilly's sister. She was fifteen and when she wasn't bored, she was mad. "Did you know that the pit bull is the world's dumbest dog?" Nilly asked. "It's so dumb that when it takes food from the dwarf poodle, which happens to be the world's smartest dog, it doesn't get that it's been tricked."

"Shut up," Eva said.

But Nilly didn't shut up. "When the dwarf poodle knows the pit bull smells bread and salami and she's coming to take it away from him, he usually smears slime from elephant snails on the bottom of the slice of bread."

"Elephant snails?" Eva scoffed, eyeing him with suspicion. Unfortunately for her, Nilly read books and thus knew quite a few things she didn't know, so Eva could never be totally sure if what he was saying was a Nilly invention or something from one of those old books of their grandfather's. For example, this might be something from the book Nilly read the most, a thick, dusty one called *Animals You Wish Didn't Exist.*

"Haven't you ever seen an elephant snail?" Nilly yelled. "All you have to do is look out the window — there's a ton of them in the lawn. Big, ooky ones. When you squish them between two books, something oozes out of them that looks like the yellowish-green snot that runs out of the noses of people who have grade-three Beijing influenza. There's no snot worse than authentic third-degree Beijing snot. Well, apart from elephant-snail slime, that is."

"If you lie anymore, you're going to go to hell," Eva said, sneaking a quick peek at the bottom of the slice of bread.

Nilly hopped down from the chair. "Fine with me,

as long as they have a band there," he said, "and I get to play the trumpet."

"You're never going to get to play in any band!" Eva yelled after him. "No one wants a trumpet player who's so small, he doesn't even come up to the top of the bass drum. No band has uniforms that small!"

Nilly put on the itty-bitty shoes that were sitting in the hallway and went out onto the front steps, stood to attention, pressed his lips together, placed them against the trumpet and blew a tune his grandfather had taught him. It was called "Morning Reveille" and was designed to wake up sleepyheads.

"Attention!" Nilly yelled when he was done, because his grandfather had taught him that too. "I want to see both feet on deck and eyes front! Everyone ready for morning inspection, fall in and prepare for the playing of the royal anthem. *Attention*!"

The movers obeyed, snapping to attention on

the gravel walkway and standing stiffly with Nilly's mum's five-seater oak sofa between them. For a few seconds it was so quiet that all you could hear were cautious birds singing and a garbage truck that was making its way up Cannon Avenue.

"Interesting," Nilly heard a jovial, accented voice say. "There's a new Commandant on the street."

Nilly turned around. A tall, thin man was leaning against the wooden fence of the house next door. His white hair was just as long and unkempt as the grass in his garden. He was wearing a blue coat like the one the woodwork teacher at Nilly's last school had worn and he was also wearing something that looked liked swimming goggles. Nilly thought he was either a Santa Claus who'd lost weight or a crazy professor.

"Was I bothering you?" Nilly asked.

"Quite the contrary," the bushy-haired man said. "I came to see who was playing so well. The sound brought back wonderful memories of a boat trip on a river in France many, many years ago."

"A boat?" Nilly asked.

"Precisely." The man closed his eyes dreamily, facing the sun. "A riverboat that was carrying me, my beloved, my motorcycle and a bunch of goats. The sun was just starting to set, the wind was picking up, the water was a little choppy, and then the goats started bleating so vigorously. I'll never forget the sound."

"Hi," Nilly said. "I'm Nilly. I'm not sure what to say to that."

"No need to say anything," the man replied. "Unless you want to say something, of course."

And that's how Nilly met Doctor Proctor. Doctor Proctor wasn't Santa Claus. But he *was* kind of crazy.

The First Powder Test

"I'M DOCTOR PROCTOR," the professor said at last. His accent was guttural, making his voice sound like a badly oiled lawnmower. "I'm a crazy professor. Well, almost, anyway." He laughed a hearty, snorting sort of laugh and started watering his unmowed lawn with a green watering can.

Nilly, who was never one to say no to an interesting conversation, set down his trumpet, ran down his front steps and over to the fence, and asked, "And just what makes you so sure that you're almost crazy, Mr Proctor?"

"*Doctor* Proctor. Did you ever hear of a professor trying to invent a powder to prevent hay fever, but ending up inventing a farting powder instead? No, I didn't think so. Quite a failure . . . and pretty outrageous, isn't it?"

"Well, it depends," Nilly said, hopping up to sit on the fence. "What does your farting powder do? Does it keep people from farting?"

The professor laughed even louder. "Ah, if only it did. I could probably have found someone to buy my powder, then," he said. Suddenly he stopped watering the grass and stroked his chin, lost in thought. "You're on to something there, Nilly. If I'd made the powder so it kept people from farting, then people could take it before going to parties or funerals. After all there are lots of occasions when farting is inappropriate. I hadn't thought of that." He dropped the watering can in the grass and hurried off towards his little blue house. "Interesting," he mumbled. "Maybe I can just reverse the formula and create a non-fart powder."

"Wait!" Nilly yelled. "Wait, Doctor Proctor."

Nilly jumped down from the fence, tumbling into the tall grass and when he got up again, he couldn't see the professor – just his blue house and a side staircase that led down to an open cellar door. Nilly ran to the door as fast as his short legs could carry him. It was dark inside, but he could hear clattering and banging. Nilly knocked hard on the door frame.

"Come in!" the professor yelled from inside.

Nilly walked into the dimly lit cellar. He could vaguely make out an old, dismantled motorcycle with a sidecar by one wall. And a shelf with various Mickey Mouse figurines and a jar full of

a light-green powder, with a label in big letters that read DR PROCTOR'S LIGHT-GREEN POWDER! and underneath, in slightly smaller letters: "A bright idea that may make the world a little more fun."

"Is this the fart powder?" Nilly asked.

"No, it's just a phosphorescent powder that makes you glow," said Doctor Proctor from somewhere in the darkness. "A rather unsuccessful invention."

Then the professor emerged from the darkness with a lit torch in one hand and a snorkel mask in the other. "Wear this for safety during the experiment. I've reversed the process so that everything goes backwards. Shut the door and watch out. Everything is connected to the light switch."

Nilly put on the face mask and pulled the door shut.

"Thanks," the professor said, flipping the light switch. The light came on and a bunch of iron pipes that ran back and forth between a bunch of barrels, tanks, tubing, funnels, test tubes and glass containers started trembling and groaning and rumbling and sputtering.

"Remember to duck if you hear a bang!" Doctor Proctor shouted over the noise. The glass containers had started simmering and boiling and smoking.

"Okay!" Nilly yelled and right then and there was a bang.

The bang was so loud that Nilly felt like earwax was being pressed into his head while at the same time his eyes were being pressed out. The light went off and it was pitch-black. And totally silent. Nilly found the torch on the floor and shone it on the professor, who was lying on his stomach with his hands over his head. Nilly tried to say something, but when he couldn't hear his own voice, he realised he had gone deaf. He stuck his right index finger into his left ear and twisted it around. Then he tried talking again. Now he could just barely hear something far away, as if there were a layer of elephant-snail slime covering his eardrum.

"That was the loudest thing I've ever heard!" he screamed.

"Eureka!" Doctor Proctor yelled, leaping up, brushing off his coat and pulling off the glasses that Nilly now realised weren't swimming goggles, but motorcycle goggles. The professor's whole face was coated in blackish-grey powder, except for two white rings where his goggles had been. Then he dashed over to one of the test tubes and poured the contents into a glass container with a strainer on top.

"Look!" Doctor Proctor exclaimed.

Nilly saw that there was a fine, light-blue powder left in the strainer. The professor stuck a teaspoon into the powder and then into his mouth. "Mmm," he said. "No change in the flavour." Then he gritted his teeth and closed his eyes. Nilly could see the professor's face slowly turning red underneath the black soot.

"What are you doing?" Nilly asked.

"I'm trying to fart," the professor hissed through his clenched teeth. "And it's not working. Isn't it great?"

He smiled as he tried one more time. But as we all know, it's very hard to smile and fart at the same time, so Doctor Proctor gave up.

"Finally I've invented something that can be used for something," he said, smiling. "An anti-fart powder."

"Can I try?" Nilly asked, nodding towards the strainer.

"You?" the professor asked, looking at Nilly. The professor raised one bushy eyebrow and lowered the other bushy eyebrow so that Nilly could tell he didn't like the idea.

"I've tested anti-fart powder before," Nilly quickly added.

"Oh, really?" the professor asked. "Where?"

"In Prague," Nilly said.

"Really? How did it go?" the professor asked.

"Fine," Nilly replied, "but I farted."

"Good," the professor said.

"What's good?" Nilly asked.

"That you farted. That means there isn't anything that *prevents* farting yet." He passed the spoon to Nilly. "Go ahead. Take it."

Nilly filled the spoon and swallowed a mouthful.

"Well?" the professor asked.

"Just a minute," Nilly mumbled with his mouth full of powder. "It sure is dry."

"Try this," the professor said, holding out a bottle.

Nilly put the bottle to his lips and washed the powder down.

"Whoa, that's good," Nilly said, looking in vain for a label on the bottle. "What is this?"

"Doctor Proctor's pear soda," the professor said. "Mostly water and sugar with a little dash of wormwood, elephant-snail slime and carbonation. . . Is something wrong?"

The professor looked worriedly at Nilly, who had suddenly started coughing violently.

"No, no," said Nilly, his eyes tearing up. "It's just that I didn't think elephant snails really existed . . ."

Bang!

Nilly looked up, frightened. The bang wasn't as loud as the first one that had made him deaf for a minute, but this time Nilly had felt a strong tug on the seat of his trousers and the cellar door had blown open.

"Oh, no!" Doctor Proctor said, hiding his face in his hands.

"What was that?" Nilly asked.

"You farrrrrrted!" the professor yelled.

"That was a fart?" Nilly whispered. "If it was, that's the loudest fart I've ever heard."

"It must be the pear soda," the professor said. "I should have known the mixture could be explosive."

Nilly started filling the spoon with more powder, but Doctor Proctor stopped him.

"I'm sorry, this isn't appropriate for children," he said.

"Sure it is," Nilly said. "All kids like to fart."

"That's absurd," Doctor Proctor said. "Farts smell bad."

"But these farts don't smell," Nilly said.

The professor sniffed loudly. "Mmm," he said. "Interesting, they don't smell."

"Do you know what this invention could be used for?" Nilly asked.

"No," Doctor Proctor said, which was the truth. "Do you?"

"Yes," Nilly said triumphantly. He crossed his arms and looked up at Doctor Proctor. "I do."

And that was the beginning of what would become Doctor Proctor's Fart Powder.

But now Nilly's mother was standing on the steps, yelling that he had to hurry because this was his first day at his new school. And that's what the next chapter is about.

The New Boy in
Mrs Strobe's Class

THE BIRDS WERE chirping and the sun was shining outside the classroom, but inside it was very quiet. Mrs Strobe nudged her glasses down her unbelievably long nose and peered at the new boy.

"So, you're Nilly then?" she said in a slow, raspy voice.

"Yup, what of it?" Nilly responded.

A few people laughed, but when Mrs Strobe did her signature move, slapping her hand against her desk, it got very quiet again in an instant.

"Could you please stand up straight, Nilly," her voice rasped. "I can hardly see you sitting there behind your desk."

"I'm sorry, Mrs Strobe," Nilly said. "But I *am* sitting up straight. The problem, as you can see, is that I'm tiny."

Now the other students were laughing even louder.

"Silence!" Mrs Strobe fumed. She nudged her glasses even further down her nose, which she could safely do because there was still plenty of nose left to go. "Since you're new, why don't you please tell us all a little bit about yourself, Mr Nilly?"

Nilly looked around. "New?" he said. "I'm not new. If you ask me, you guys are the ones who are new. Apart from Lisa, that is. I've met her already."

Everyone turned around to look at Lisa, who mostly wanted to sink down on to the floor.

"Besides, I'm ten years old," Nilly said. "So, for example, if I were a pair of shoes, I wouldn't be new at all. I'd be extremely old. My grandfather had a dog who got sent to the old age home when she was ten."

Mrs Strobe didn't make any attempt to stop the snide laughter that followed, but just looked at Nilly thoughtfully until the laughter had subsided.

"Enough clowning around, Mr Nilly," she said, a thin smile spreading over her thin lips. "Considering your modest size, I suggest that you stand on your desk while you address the class."

To Mrs Strobe's surprise, Nilly didn't wait to be asked twice, but leaped up on to his desk and hoisted his trouser up by his braces.

"I live on Cannon Avenue with my sister and mother. We've lived in every county in Norway, plus a couple that aren't in Norway anymore. By which I

mean, they were in Norway during the Ice Age, but once the ice started melting, big pieces broke off and drifted away in the ocean. One of the biggest pieces is called America now and over there they have no idea that they're living on a chunk of ice that used to be part of Norway."

"Mr Nilly," Mrs Strobe interrupted. "Stick to the most important details, please."

"The most important," Nilly said, "is playing the trumpet in the Norwegian Independence Day parade on the seventeenth of May. Because playing the trumpet is like kissing a woman. Can anyone tell me where I can find the nearest marching band?"

But everyone in the classroom just stared at him with their mouths hanging open.

"Oh, yeah. I almost forgot," Nilly said. "I was there this morning when one of the world's greatest inventions was invented. The inventor's name is Doctor Proctor and I was selected to be his assistant.

We're calling the invention Doctor Proctor's Far—"

"Enough!" Mrs Strobe yelled. "You can take your seat, Mr Nilly."

Mrs Strobe spent the rest of the class explaining the history of Norwegian Independence Day, but none of the children in the classroom were listening. They were just staring at the little bit of Nilly they could see sticking up over his desk. Then the bell rang.

DURING BREAK-TIME NILLY stood by himself watching the other children play tag and hopscotch. He noticed Lisa, who was also just standing there watching. Nilly was just about to go over to her when two large boys with crew cuts and barrel-shaped heads suddenly stepped in front of him, blocking his way. Nilly already had an idea of what was coming next.

"Hello, pip-squeak," one of them said.

"Hello, O giants who wander the earth with heavy

footsteps, blocking out the sun," Nilly said without looking up.

"Huh?" the boy said.

"Nothing, pit bulls," Nilly said.

"You're new," the other boy said.

"So what?" Nilly asked quietly. Even though he already knew more or less what the answer to the so-what question would be.

"New means we dunk you in the drinking fountain," the other boy said.

"Why?" Nilly asked, even more quietly. He knew the answer to that too.

The first boy shrugged. "Because . . . because . . ." he started, trying to think of the reason. And then all three of them – the two boys and Nilly, that is – all exclaimed in unison: *"Because that's just the way it is."*

The two boys looked around, obviously checking if any of the teachers were nearby. Then the bigger of the two boys grabbed Nilly's collar and lifted him up. The other one took hold of Nilly's legs, and then they carried him off towards the drinking fountain in the middle of the playground. Nilly hung there like a limp sack of flour between those two, studying a little white cloud that looked like an overfed rhinoceros up in the breathtakingly blue sky. He could hear children joining the procession, mumbling quietly in anticipation. He watched them fight for a chance to plug the openings of the other fountains with their fingers so that only one, powerful stream of water was left, shooting almost three metres into the air. Nilly felt himself being lifted up and could feel the cold gust of air next to the stream of water. People started cheering.

"We christen you . . ." said the guy holding Nilly's legs.

"Flame Head the Pygmy," the other said.

"Nice one, dude!" the first one yelled. "Guess we'd better put out his flame!"

The boys laughed so hard, it made Nilly shake up and down. Then they held him over the fountain of water, which shot Nilly right in the face, hitting his nose and mouth. He couldn't breathe and for a second he thought he was going to drown, but then the hands lifted him up out of the stream. Nilly looked around at all the children near the drinking fountains and at Lisa, who was still standing by herself at the edge of the playground.

"More, more!" the kids yelled. Nilly sighed and took a deep breath. Then they dunked him down into the water again.

Nilly didn't put up any opposition and didn't say a word. He just closed his eyes and mouth. He tried to imagine he was sitting at the front of his grandfather's motorboat with his head hanging out over the side, so the sea spray hit him in the face.

When the boys were done, they set Nilly down again and went on their way. Nilly's wet red hair stuck to his

head and his shoes squished. The other kids crowded around and watched, laughing at him, while Nilly pulled his T-shirt up from between the braces.

"Weak drinking fountains you guys have here," he said loudly.

It got awfully quiet around him. Nilly dried his face. "At Trafalgar Square in London they have a drinking fountain that shoots ten metres straight up," he said. "A friend of mine tried to drink from it. The water knocked out two teeth and he swallowed his own retainer. We saw an Italian guy get his wig knocked off when he went to take a drink."

Nilly paused dramatically as he wrung out his wet T-shirt. "True, some people said it wasn't a wig, that it was the Italian guy's own hair that had been pulled right out. I decided to try sitting on the fountain." Nilly leaned to the side to get the water out of his ear.

Finally one of the kids asked, "What happened?"

"Well," Nilly said, holding his nose and blowing

hard, first through one nostril and then the other.

"What did he say?" one of the kids who was standing farther back asked. The ones who were standing in front said, "Shhh!"

"From up where I was sitting, I could see all the way to France, which was more than five hundred miles away," Nilly said, shaking his bangs and sending out a spray of water. "That may sound like an exaggeration," he said, pulling a comb out of his back pocket and running it through his hair. "But you have to remember that it was an unusually clear day and that that part of Europe is extremely flat."

Then Nilly plowed his way through the crowd of kids and walked over to Lisa at the edge of the playground.

"Well," she said with a little smile. "What do you think of our school so far?"

"Not so bad," he said. "No one's called me Silly Nilly yet."

"Those two were Truls and Trym," Lisa said. "They're twins and, unfortunately, they live on Cannon Avenue."

Nilly shrugged. "Truls and Trym live everywhere."

"What do you mean?" Lisa asked.

"Every street has Trulses and Tryms. You can't get away from them, no matter where you move," Nilly explained.

Lisa thought about it. Could there be Trulses and Tryms in Sarpsborg too?

"Did you find a new best friend yet?" Nilly asked.

Lisa shook her head. They stood there next to each other in silence, watching the other kids play, until Lisa asked, "Was that really true, what you said about Doctor Proctor and the invention?"

"Of course," Nilly said with a wry smile. "Almost everything I say is true."

Right then the bell rang.

Nilly Has an Idea

THAT AFTERNOON NILLY knocked hard on the cellar door at the blue house. Three firm knocks. That was the signal they'd agreed on.

Doctor Proctor flung open the door and when he saw Nilly, he exclaimed, "Wonderful!" Then he raised one bushy eyebrow and lowered another bushy eyebrow, pointed, and asked, "Who is that?"

"Lisa," Nilly said.

"I can see that," the professor said. "She lives across the street if I'm not mistaken. What I mean is: what's she doing here? Didn't we agree that this project was top secret?"

"Obviously it's not that secret," Lisa said. "Nilly told the whole class about it today."

"What?" the professor exclaimed, frightened. "Nilly, is that true?"

"Uh," Nilly said. "A little, maybe."

"You told . . . you told . . ." the professor sputtered, waving his arms around in the air, while Nilly stuck out his lower lip and made his eyes look big, as if he were on the verge of tears. This facial expression, which Nilly had practised especially for situations like this, made him look like a tiny, little, very depressed camel. Because everyone knows that it's absolutely impossible to be mad at a very depressed camel. The professor groaned, giving up, and lowered his arms again. "Well, well, maybe it's not so terrible. And you are my assistant after all, so I suppose it's all right."

"Thanks," Nilly said quietly.

"Sure, sure," said the professor, waving his hands at Nilly. "You can stop trying to look like a camel now. Come in and close the door behind you."

They did as he said, while Doctor Proctor hurried over to the test tubes and glass containers that were bubbling and smoking with something that smelled like cooked pears.

Lisa stopped just inside the door and looked around. There was a potted plant with white petals on the windowsill. And on the wall next to it hung a picture of a motorcycle with a sidecar in front of what she assumed must be the Eiffel Tower in Paris. A smiling young man who looked like the professor was sitting on the motorcycle seat and there was a sweet, smiling girl with dark hair in the sidecar.

"What are you doing?" Nilly asked Doctor Proctor.

"I'm perfecting the product," he said, stirring some mixture in a big barrel. "Something that ought to give it even more pep. A concoction of the more explosive type, you might say."

The professor dipped a finger in and then brought it to his mouth. "Hmm. A little more wormwood."

"Can I taste?" Lisa asked, peering over the edge of the barrel.

"Sorry," the professor said.

"Sorry," Nilly said.

"Why not?" Lisa asked.

"Are you a certified fart powder tester, perhaps?" Nilly asked.

Lisa thought for a second and said, "Not as far as I know."

"Then I recommend that you leave the testing to me for the time being," Nilly said, pulling on his braces. Then he took a spoon and stuck it down into the barrel.

"Careful," the professor said. "Start with a quarter of a spoonful."

"Sure," Nilly said, putting a quarter spoonful of powder in his mouth.

"Then we'll start the countdown," Doctor Proctor said and looked at the clock. "Seven – six – five – four – three . . . hey, don't stand right behind him, Lisa!"

Right then there was a bang. And Lisa felt a blast of air hitting her before she lost her balance and sat down hard on her bottom on the cold floor.

"Oh," Nilly said. "Lisa, are you okay?"

"Yeah," she said, a little dazed as the professor helped her back on to her feet. "Well, I'd call that some pep!"

Nilly laughed out loud. "Well done, Doctor!"

"Thank you, thank you," the professor said. "I think I'll conduct a little test myself . . ."

The professor took half a teaspoon and counted down. At zero there was another bang, but this time Lisa was careful to stand by the door.

"Wow," the professor said, picking up the plant, which didn't have leaves on it anymore. "I think we'll do the next test outside."

They poured the powder into a biscuit tin and brought it outside.

"Give me the teaspoon," Nilly said.

"Careful with the dose . . ." Doctor Proctor started to say, but Nilly had already gobbled up a full teaspoon.

"I feel a tingling in my stomach," said Nilly, who

was so excited that he was whining and jumping up and down.

"Seven – six – five," the professor counted.

When the bang came, all the songbirds in the professor's pear tree took off and flew away in alarm. And this time it wasn't Lisa but Nilly who got knocked over and disappeared in the tall grass.

"Where are you?" Doctor Proctor yelled, searching in the grass. "How did it go?"

They heard a gurgling noise and then Nilly popped up, totally red in the face from laughing.

"More!" he yelled. "More!"

"Look, Professor!" Lisa pointed. "It ripped the seat of Nilly's trousers!"

And indeed it had. Nilly's trousers were practically torn apart. The professor looked at the results with concern and decided that they should stop the testing for today. He asked them to search for his lawn furniture, which was in the grass somewhere, and then went inside. When he came back out he brought bread, butter, liverwurst and juice. Lisa had found the lawn furniture and while they sat in the crooked white-painted chairs and ate, they contemplated what the invention could be used for. The professor had the idea of trying to sell the powder to farmers. "They could eat a half teaspoon of fart powder," he explained, "and hold the sack of seed grain in front of the . . . uh, launch site. Then the air pressure would spread the seeds over the whole field. It'll save a ton of time. What do you guys think?"

"Excellent!" Nilly said.

"To be completely honest," Lisa said, "I don't think people are really going to want to eat food that comes from seeds that have been farted on."

"Hmm," the professor said, scratching his mop of white hair. "You're probably right about that."

"What about making the world's fastest bicycle pump?" Nilly yelled. "All you have to do is take a hose, fasten one end to your bum and the other to the valve on the bike tyre and then . . . *kaboom!* The tyre is filled in a fraction of a second!"

"Interesting," said the professor, stroking his goatee. "But I'm afraid it's the kaboom that's the problem. The tyre's going to explode too."

"What if we use the fart powder to dry hair?" Lisa suggested.

Nilly and the professor looked at Lisa while she explained that the whole family could draw straws, everyone from the littlest to Grandma, to see who would eat the fart powder after everyone had showered in the morning. And then everyone else could just stand behind that person.

"Good idea," said the professor. "But who's going to dry the farter's hair?"

"And what if the blast knocks Grandma over and she breaks her hip?" Nilly said.

They kept tossing out one suggestion after

another, but all of the suggestions had some kind of annoying drawback or other. In the end they were all sitting there quietly chewing their sandwiches when Nilly suddenly exclaimed, "I have it!"

Lisa and Doctor Proctor looked at him without much enthusiasm, since this was the fourth time in only a couple of minutes that Nilly had said he had it and so far he definitely hadn't had it. Nilly leaped up on to the table. "We could just use the powder for the same thing we've been using it for so far!" he said.

"But we're not using it for anything," the professor said.

"We're just making meaningless bangs," Lisa said.

"Exactly!" Nilly said. "And who likes meaningless bangs better than anything?"

"Well," the professor said. "Kids, I guess. And adults who are a little childish."

"Exactly! And when do they want things that bang?"

"New Year's Eve?"

"Yes!" Nilly shouted, excited. "And . . . and . . . and?"

"Norwegian Independence Day!" Lisa blurted out, jumping up on to the table next to Nilly. "That's only a few days away! Don't you see, Professor? We don't need to come up with anything at all, we can just sell the powder the way it is!"

The professor's eyes widened and he stretched his thin, wrinkled neck so that he looked like some kind of shorebird. "Interesting," he mumbled. "Very interesting. Independence Day . . . children . . . things that go boom . . . it's . . . it's . . ." With a bounce he leaped up on to the table too. "Eureka!"

And as if on cue the three of them started dancing a victory dance around the table.

Conductor Madsen and the Dølgen School Marching Band

MR MADSEN WAS standing in the gym with both arms out in front of him. Facing him sat the twenty students who made up the Dølgen School Marching Band. Mr Madsen squeezed a baton between his right thumb and index finger, his other eight fingers splayed in all directions. He had closed his eyes and for a second he imagined he was far away from the bleachers, worn-wood floor and stinky gym mats, standing before a sold-out audience in a concert hall in Venice, with chandeliers hanging from the ceiling and cheering people in formal clothes in the balcony seats. Then Mr Madsen opened his eyes again.

"Ready?" he yelled, wrinkling his nose so his dark sunglasses wouldn't slide down. Because unlike Mrs Strobe, Mr Madsen had a short, fat nose with black pores.

None of the twenty faces in the chairs in front of him looked like they were ready. But they didn't protest either so Mr Madsen counted down as if for a rocket launch.

"Four – three – two – one!"

Then Mr Madsen swung his baton as if it were a magic wand and the Dølgen School Marching Band began to play. Not like a rocket, exactly. More like a train that, snorting and puffing, started to move. As usual, the drums had started playing long before Mr Madsen got to "one." Now he was just waiting for the rest of the band. First came a screech of a trombone, then a French horn bleated in the wrong key, before two clarinets played almost the same note. The two trumpet players, the twins Truls and Trym Trane, were picking their noses. Finally Petra managed to get her tuba to make a sound and Per made a hesitant tap on the base drum.

"No, no, no!" Mr Madsen called, losing hope and waving his baton defensively. But just like a train, the Dølgen School Marching Band was hard to stop once it got going. And when they tried to stop, it sounded like a ton of kitchen implements falling on the floor. *Crash! Bang! Toooot!* When it was finally quiet and the windows at Dølgen School had stopped vibrating, Mr Madsen took off his sunglasses.

"My dear ladies and gentlemen," he said. "Do

you know how many days there are left until Independence Day?"

No one said anything.

Mr Madsen groaned. "Well, I wouldn't expect you to either, since you don't even seem to know what song we're playing. What song is this, Trym?"

Trym stopped picking his nose and glanced over at his brother questioningly.

"Well, Truls," Mr Madsen said. "Can you help Trym out?"

Truls scratched his back with his trumpet and squinted at the music stand. "I've got some rain on my music, Mr Madsen. I can't see nothin'," he said.

"Right," Mr Madsen said. "For crying out loud, this is the national anthem. Is there really no one here besides Lisa who can read music? Or at least play in key?"

Lisa cowered behind her clarinet as she felt everyone else looking at her. She knew what those looks were saying. They were saying that even if Mr Madsen said she was good, she shouldn't think that any of them wanted to be friends with her. In fact, the opposite was true.

"If we don't improve by Independence Day, we're going to have to give up the idea of a band camp this summer," Mr Madsen said. "I don't want to be made into a laughing stock in front of dozens of other band conductors. Understood?"

Mr Madsen saw the faces in front of him start gaping. This was a shock to them, that much was clear. After all he had talked so much and so positively about the big band competition in Eidsvoll and they were all really looking forward to it. But he had made it clear to them from the very beginning. Nikolai Amadeus Madsen was not playing around, conducting a rattling, old military band. So unless a miracle occurred, no one at Eidsvoll was going to hear so much as a triangle clang from the Dølgen School Marching Band. And unfortunately, since Mr Madsen's baton wasn't a magic wand, there wasn't going to be any miracle.

"Let's take it again from the top," Mr Madsen said with a sigh, raising his baton. "Ready?"

But they simply were not ready. In fact, they were all staring at the door to the locker room that was right behind Mr Madsen's back. Irritated he turned around but he couldn't see anyone. He turned back towards the band and was just about to count off when his brain realised that it had seen something in the doorway after all. Something down by the floor. He turned around, took off his sunglasses and looked at the tiny little boy with the red hair.

"What are you doing here?" Mr Madsen asked curtly.

"Shouldn't you ask *who* I am first?" Nilly said, holding out an old, beaten-up trumpet. "I'm Nilly. I can play the trumpet. You want to hear me play a little?"

"No!" Mr Madsen said.

"Just a little . . ." Nilly said, raising his trumpet and forming his lips as if for a kiss.

"No! No! No!" growled Mr Madsen, who was bright red in the face and slapping his thigh with the baton. "I am an artist!" he yelled. "I have arranged marches for the big marching-band festival in Venice. And now I'm conducting a school band for tone-deaf brats and I don't need to hear one more tone-deaf brat. Understood? Now get out!"

"Hmm," Nilly said. "That sounded like an A. I have perfect pitch. Just check with your tuning fork."

"You're not only tone-deaf, you're deaf!" Mr Madsen sputtered, shaking and spitting in agitation. "Shut that door again and don't ever come back here! Surely you don't think any band would take someone so small that . . . that . . ."

"That there isn't even room for the stripe on the side of his uniform trousers," Nilly said. "So short that his band medals would drag on the ground. So teensy-weensy that he couldn't see what was on the music stand. Whose uniform hat would fall down over his eyes."

Nilly smiled innocently at Mr Madsen, who was now rushing straight towards him in long strides.

"So he can't see where he's going," Nilly continued. "And suddenly he finds himself on Aker Street while the rest of the band is marching down Karl Johan Street."

"Exactly!" Mr Madsen said, grabbing hold of the door and flinging it shut right in Nilly's face. Then he stomped back over to his music stand. He noted the big grins on Truls and Trym's faces before he raised his baton.

"So," Mr Madsen said. "Back to the national anthem."

That Night, in a Sewer Beneath Oslo

THERE ARE BIG animals in the sewers that run every which way beneath Oslo. So big that you probably wouldn't want to bump into them. But if you pick up a manhole cover on one of Oslo's streets and shine a torch down into the sewer world, it just might happen that you'll see the light catch the teeth in the jaws of one of the huge, slimy beasts before it scurries away. Or before it sinks its teeth into your throat. Because they are quite speedy beasts. And we're not talking now about the regular, innocent *Rattus norvegicus* i.e. little Norwegian rats, but about properly beastly beasts. Like Attila. Attila was an old Mongolian water vole who'd lived for thirty-five years and weighed more than fourteen kilograms. If you want to read more about water voles, turn to page 678 of *Animals You Wish Didn't Exist.*

As it so happened, Attila liked to eat a little *Rattus norvegicus* for breakfast and was the king of the Oslo Municipal Sewer and Drainage System. That is to say, Attila thought it was, until now. Attila's reign had started many years ago, but this water vole hadn't always been king. When Attila was a few months old and was a cute, tiny fur ball weighing only a few grams, it had been bought in a pet store by a family in Hovseter, Norway. They bought the Mongolian water vole because the fat little boy in the family had pointed at Attila and yelled that he wanted a rat like that. And his parents had done what the little boy ordered. They had fed Attila fish balls, the worst thing Attila knew of, and put a metal collar on the rat with the name ATTILA engraved on it, and the fat little boy had tormented the poor water vole every single day by poking sticks into the cage. Every single day, until the day Attila had got so big from eating fish balls that it needed a new cage while it could still fit through the opening of the old one. Attila had been looking forward to this day. And when the boy stuck his hand into the cage to drag Attila out, Attila had opened its mouth as wide as it could and sunk its teeth into the delicious, soft, white human meat. This was a totally different kind of meatball! And while the little boy screamed and his blood gushed, Attila was out of the cage, as fast as a Mongolian water vole could go, out of the house, away from the above-ground part of Hovseter and down into the sewer. And from there the water vole had found his way to downtown Oslo, where its beastly behaviour had quickly earned the water vole respect. Attila was feared by Norwegian rats citywide, from the manhole covers at Majorstua subway station to the sewage treatment plant at Aker.

But on this night, deep beneath Oslo, while Lisa and Nilly were sleeping like babies, it was Attila who was gripped by fear. The vole was sitting in the corner of a sewer pipe, shaking. Because in a flash of light it had seen something right in front of him. A glimpse of teeth. Teeth even bigger than its own. Could the legend he'd been hearing for all these years in the Oslo Municipal Sewer and Drainage System be true after all? Attila felt its Mongolian water vole heart pounding in fear and it was so dark, so dark. And for the first time Attila realised that it actually smelled pretty bad down here in the sewer and that it really would prefer to be anywhere else besides this sewer pipe right now. Even its old cage in Hovseter. So Attila tried to comfort itself. Obviously the legend must be made up. An anaconda? What rubbish. An anaconda is a boa constrictor that is found in the Amazon, where it lives off of huge water voles and such, not here deep beneath Oslo, where there aren't any water voles at all. Apart from the one, that is. Attila contemplated this briefly.

And while Attila was thinking, something moved towards the water vole. It was huge, like an inflatable swimming ring, surrounded by jagged teeth the size of ice-cream cones, and it was hissing and had such bad breath that the rest of the sewer smelled like a flower bed in comparison.

It was so frightening that Attila quite simply squeezed its eyes shut.

When the vole opened them again something was dripping and dripping all around. And it was excessively dark. Just as if Attila weren't sitting in a sewer pipe, but inside something that was even darker. And it was as if the walls were moving, pulling in closer and slithering. As if the water vole were already inside the stomach of . . . of . . .

Attila screamed at least as loud as that fat little boy he had bitten so long ago.

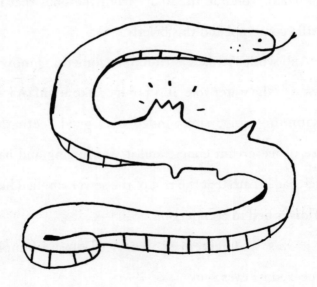

Nilly Does Simple Maths

WHEN LISA WALKED out the door the next morning, Nilly was standing across the street with his backpack on, kicking rocks.

"What are you waiting for?" Lisa asked.

Nilly shrugged and said, "To see if anyone walks by who's going the same way as me."

"No one's going to come by," Lisa said. "This is a dead-end street and we live at the end of it."

"Well then," Nilly said, and they started walking down Cannon Avenue together.

"Proctor invited us to come over after school for the Last Big Powder Test," Nilly said. "Are you coming?"

"Of course," Lisa said. "Are you excited?"

"As excited as a little kid," said Nilly.

When they'd made it almost all the way down to the main road Lisa stopped and pointed at the house at the bottom of Cannon Avenue.

"That's where Truls and Trym live," she said. "If I see them come out, I usually wait here until they're gone. If I don't see them, I run quickly past. Come on . . ."

Lisa took Nilly's hand and was about to run, but Nilly held her back.

"I don't want to run," he said. "And I don't want to wait either."

"But . . ." Lisa began.

"Remember, there's two of us," Nilly said. "There's just as many of us as Truls and Trym. At least. It's simple maths."

So they walked past Truls and Trym's house. Nilly was walking really, really slowly, Lisa thought. She could still tell that he was a little scared though, because he was constantly looking over at the house. But luckily neither Truls nor Trym came out and Lisa looked at her watch and realised they must have gone to school already.

"Do you know what time it is?" she exclaimed in alarm, because she was a good girl and wasn't used to being late.

"I don't have a watch," Nilly said.

"Mrs Strobe is going to be super angry. Hurry!"

"Aye, aye, boss," Nilly said.

And they ran so fast that they got there in the time it took you to read from the beginning of this chapter to here.

UNFORTUNATELY TIME DIDN'T pass as quickly the rest of the day. Nilly was so impatient to get home for the Last Big Powder Test that he sat there in the classroom counting the seconds as he watched Mrs Strobe's mouth moving. He wasn't paying attention, so when he suddenly realised that Mrs Strobe was pointing at him and that everyone else in class was looking at him, Nilly figured that Mrs Strobe had probably asked him a question.

"Two thousand six hundred and eighty-one," Nilly said.

Mrs Strobe wrinkled her brow and asked, "Is that supposed to be the answer to my question?"

"Not necessarily," Nilly said. "But that's how

many seconds have passed during this class. Well, now four more have gone by, so now two thousand six hundred and eighty-five seconds have passed. It's simple maths."

"I understand that," Mrs Strobe started. "But Nilly . . ."

"Excuse me. That isn't the right answer anymore," Nilly said. "The right answer is now two thousand six hundred and eighty-nine."

"To me it sounds like you're trying to talk your way out of what I asked you about," Mrs Strobe said. "Because you heard what I asked you, right, Nilly?"

"Of course," Nilly said. "Two thousand six hundred and ninety-two."

"Get to the point," Mrs Strobe said, sounding a little irritated now.

"The point," Nilly said, "is that since there are sixty seconds in a minute and forty-five minutes in each class, I won't have time to answer your question, since sixty seconds times forty-five is two thousand seven hundred seconds, and that means the bell is going to ring right . . ."

No one heard the rest of what Nilly said, because the bell started ringing right then, loud and shrill. Mrs Strobe tried looking sternly at Nilly, but when she yelled, "All right, everyone out!" he could see that she couldn't quite help but smile anyway.

AFTER LISA AND Nilly had spent sixteen thousand and two hundred seconds together in the classroom and two thousand seven hundred seconds on the playground, they ran away from the school as quickly as they had run towards it. They parted on Cannon Avenue, each opening their own gate, each running up their own front steps and each flinging their backpack in their own hallway. Then they met again in front of Doctor Proctor's gate.

"I'm almost dreading it a little," Lisa said.

"I'm almost looking forward to it a little," Nilly said.

Then they stormed into the garden and through the tall grass.

"There you guys are!" called the doctor joyfully in his remarkable accent. He was sitting at the picnic table under the pear tree. In front of him lay three tablespoons and a teaspoon, an ice hockey helmet, two knee pads, a jar full of powder, a pair of motorcycle pants and a metre long, rectangular, homemade jelly bathed in caramel sauce. "Are you guys ready for the Last Big Powder Test?" he asked.

"Yes!" Lisa and Nilly shouted in unison.

"But first, jelly," said the doctor.

They sat down around the table and each grabbed a spoon.

"On your marks, get set . . ." Doctor Proctor said.

"Go!" Nilly yelled, and they flung themselves at the jelly. If Nilly had been counting, he wouldn't have got any further than thirty seconds before the metre long jelly had vanished completely.

"Good," Nilly said, patting his stomach.

"Good," Lisa said, patting her stomach.

"I've made a few tiny adjustments to the powder mixture," Doctor Proctor said.

"I'm ready," Nilly said, taking the lid off the jar.

"Hold on!" the professor said. "I don't want you to ruin your trousers again, so I made these."

He held up the motorcycle trousers. They were very normal, aside from the fact that the seat of the trousers had a Velcro flap.

"So the air can pass through unobstructed," the doctor explained. "I remodelled my old motorcycle gear."

"Niiice," Nilly said once he'd put on the trousers,

which were way too big for him. Lisa just shook her head.

"These too," the doctor said, and passed Nilly the hockey helmet and the knee pads. "In case you get knocked over again."

Nilly put everything on, then crawled up onto the table and over to the jar.

"Only one teaspoon!" Doctor Proctor yelled.

"Yeah, yeah!" Nilly said, filling the spoon he was holding in his hand and sticking it into his mouth.

"Okay," the doctor said, looking at his watch. "We'll start the countdown then. Seven. Six."

"Doctor Proctor . . ." Lisa said warily.

"Not now, Lisa. Nilly, hop down from the table and stand over there so you don't ruin anything. Four. Three," the doctor continued.

"He didn't use the teaspoon," Lisa practically whispered.

"Two," the doctor said. "What did you say, Lisa?"

"Nilly used that big tablespoon he ate his jelly with," Lisa said.

The doctor stared at Lisa with big, horrified eyes. "One," he said. "Tablespoon?"

Lisa nodded.

"Oh, no," Doctor Proctor said, running towards Nilly.

"What now?" Lisa whispered.

"Simple maths," Nilly yelled happily. "Zero."

And then came the bang. And if the earlier bangs had been loud, they were nothing compared to this. This was as if the whole world had exploded. And the air pressure! Lisa felt her eyelids and lips distort as she was peppered with dirt and pebbles.

When her eyes settled back into place, the first thing Lisa noticed was that the birds had stopped singing. Then she noticed Doctor Proctor, who was sitting in the grass with a confused look on his face. The leaves from the big pear tree wafted down around him as if it were suddenly Autumn. But she didn't see Nilly. She looked to the right, to the left and behind her. And finally she looked up. But Nilly was nowhere to be seen. Then the first bird cautiously started singing again. And that's when it occurred to Lisa that she might never, ever see Nilly again and that that would actually be almost as sad as Anna having moved to Sarpsborg.

The Fartonaut

WHEN NILLY SAID "zero" he felt an absolutely wonderful tickle in his stomach. It was as if the fart was a giant, burbling laugh that just had to get out. Sure he had seen Lisa's worried expression and Doctor Proctor coming running towards him, but he was so excited that it hadn't occurred to him that something might be wrong. And when the bang came, it was so delightfully liberating that Nilly automatically shut his eyes. The previous farts had been short explosions, but this one was more drawn out, like when you let the air out of a balloon. Nilly laughed out loud because it felt just like he'd blasted off from the ground, like he was an astronaut who'd been shot up and propelled into space. He could feel the air rushing past his face and hair and it was as if his arms were being pressed in against his body. It felt totally real. And when Nilly finally opened his eyes he discovered that it was very real in reality too. He blinked twice and then he understood that not only was it very real, it was utterly, incredibly real. It was as if he were sitting on a chair of air that was shooting upwards. The blue sky arched above him and below him he saw a big cloud of dust in what looked like a tiny copy of Doctor Proctor's garden. The fart howled like a whole pack of wolves and Nilly

realised he was still going up, because the landscape down below was starting to look like a smaller and smaller version of Legoland.

Then the fart turned into a low rumbling, the chair of air disappeared from underneath him and for just a second, Nilly felt like he was totally weightless. A crow turned its head as it flew by, staring at him with astonished crow eyes.

Nilly tipped forwards and then felt the descent begin. Headfirst. Slowly at first, then faster.

Uh-oh, Nilly thought, no longer finding any reason to smile. *Hockey helmet or not, I'm never going to survive this.*

Legoland got bigger and bigger, and with perilous speed it started to resemble the Cannon Avenue that Nilly had just left. And things very surely would have gone really badly for our friend Nilly if he hadn't been such a quick-witted little guy and remembered what it was that had sent him up in the first place. Because although the fart was no longer howling like a pack of wolves and was now just a tame sputtering, it was still going. And remember that when I say sputtering, that's compared to an enormous bang and not compared to one of your farts. Because even if you've been eating un-ripe apples and think you just farted the loudest fart anyone has ever farted, it would be considered a gentle breeze compared to the tamest sputtering caused by Doctor Proctor's Fart Powder. Once Nilly had thought about all this, he swung himself quickly back into the sitting position he'd been in when he'd flown up. And once the seat of his trousers, with the open Velcro flap, was pointed straight at the ground, to his relief he immediately started slowing down, thanks to the air pressure of the fart. But he also knew that the fart was going to be over soon and there was still a way to go until he was back on the ground. Nilly tried as hard as he could to keep it going, because even an eight-metre fall is very high for such a small boy. And that's exactly how high he was above the ground when the fart finally came to an end.

"NILLY!" LISA YELLED.

"Nilly!" Doctor Proctor yelled. They were still looking around for him like crazy.

"Do you think the powder exploded him into smithereens?" Lisa asked.

"If so the pieces must be so small that we can't see them," Doctor Proctor said, adjusting his motorcycle glasses and studying the ground where Nilly had been standing when the fart happened. All of the grass was torn up and there was a little pit there.

"We're never going to see him again," Lisa said. "And it's my fault. I should've noticed that he was holding the tablespoon."

"No, no. It's my fault," Doctor Proctor said, getting up again. "I should never have tinkered with the formula."

"Nilly!" Lisa yelled.

"Nilly!" Doctor Proctor yelled.

"What's all the commotion?" someone complained from over by the fence along the road. "And what are you doing here, Lisa? Dinner's on the table."

It was Lisa's father, the Commandant. He looked gruff.

Doctor Proctor stood up. "My good sir, the whole situation is hopeless—" he started, but was interrupted by a voice barking from behind the fence at Nilly's house.

"What's all the commotion?" It was Nilly's mother. She looked mad. "Dinner's on the table. Has anyone seen Nilly?"

Doctor Proctor turned to face her. "My good ma'am, the whole situation is hopeless. You see, your son, Nilly, he . . . he . . ."

Then Doctor Proctor was interrupted for the third time and this time by a high-pitched boy's voice that came from above: "He's sitting up here wondering what's for dinner."

All four of them looked up. And there, on top of Doctor Proctor's roof, stood Nilly with his arms crossed, wearing a hockey helmet, knee pads and leather trousers with the bottom flapping around.

"Don't move," called Doctor Proctor, running into the cellar.

"What in the world are you doing up there, Nilly?" his mother squealed.

"Playing hide-and-seek obviously," Nilly said. "What's for dinner?"

"Meatballs," Nilly's mother said to Nilly.

"Fish au gratin," Lisa's father told Lisa.

"Yippee!" said Nilly.

"Yippee!" said Lisa.

"You guys can go back to playing after dinner," Lisa's father growled.

"But not up there," Nilly's mother said. "Get down here right now."

"Yes, Mom," Nilly said.

The doctor came running back out of the cellar with a ladder that he immediately leaned up against the wall of his house so that it was resting against the gutter. Nilly crawled to the ladder and then down the rungs, smiling and as proud as an astronaut climbing down from his spaceship after a successful landing following an expedition to somewhere in space where no one – or at least very few people – had ever been before him.

And three minutes later, which a little simple maths can tell you is the same as a hundred and eighty seconds, Lisa was sitting with freshly washed, completely clean hands, eating fish au gratin, and Nilly, with pretty clean hands, was eating meatballs. Neither of them had ever eaten so fast before.

* * *

WHEN THEY GOT back to Doctor Proctor's yard, the professor was sitting on the bench, reviewing everything as he jotted some things down and did some calculations on a piece of paper. Nilly looked at all the numbers and squiggles. This maths wasn't quite so simple.

"With the new formula the effect of the powder is seven times stronger," Proctor said in his heavy accent. "That's why I said you should use the teaspoon, not the tablespoon."

Nilly shrugged. "It worked out fine. The fart ended when I was on my way down, just as I reached the roof of your house."

"Hmm," the professor said, looking at the numbers. "But I'm puzzled about why you took off like a rocket."

"It was a looong fart," Nilly said. "It was like sitting on a column of air that was pushing me up. And it was the same column that slowed me down on the way back down too."

"Hmm," the doctor said, scratching his chin. "Because of the new formula, the powder seems to have a much longer reaction time. Interesting."

"Maybe we should go back to the original formula," Lisa suggested hesitantly.

"I suppose you're right, Lisa," the doctor said. "It would be dangerous to sell this powder mixture to children. Or adults, for that matter."

"I've got it," Nilly said. "We make two kinds of powder. A Doctor Proctor's Fart Powder that we sell to all the kids for Independence Day. And a Doctor Proctor's Rather Special Rocket Mixture that we don't sell to anyone. That we just do some tiny little tests with here in the garden."

Doctor Proctor didn't look like he liked the last part of the idea that much.

"Just every once in a while, I mean," Nilly said. "When we're really super bored."

Doctor Proctor still looked like he didn't like the idea.

"Or," Lisa said, "we could sell it to NASA."

"NASA?" Nilly and Doctor Proctor asked in unison.

"The U.S. National Aeronautics and Space Administration," Lisa said without tripping over a single syllable. "They're the ones who send astronauts into space. My dad said it costs more to build one small spaceship than all of Akershus Fortress put together. Just think how happy they'll be when they find out you can send astronauts up without a spaceship."

"Hmm," Doctor Proctor said. "Interesting."

"And maybe we could do something about the name of the rocket powder too," Lisa said. "What about Doctor Proctor's Fartonaut Powder?"

"That's it, Lisa!" Nilly yelled. "You're a genius!"

"Excellent," Doctor Proctor said. "This calls for a celebration. . . ."

And while Doctor Proctor shuffled into the house to get the other metre long portion of the jelly he'd made, Lisa beamed. Because it's always nice to be praised when you've been extra clever.

Nilly Gets Tricked and Juliette Margarine

THE NEXT DAY rumours started flying on the playground, about a powder that makes you fart louder than you ever have before. And you didn't even have to try hard. And best of all: There was absolutely no smell. Supposedly the bang was louder than thirteen firecrackers, three bangers, and a half stick of dynamite put together *and* the powder cost less than a bottle of fizzy pop. Plus it was totally harmless and was totally legal. In short, the kids at school thought it was too good to be true.

But none of them knew where they could get hold of this powder. They only knew that Lisa and Nilly, that new little kid with the red hair, knew everything they didn't know.

And Lisa and Nilly wouldn't say anything.

The other kids nagged them between each class, but Lisa just smiled slyly while Nilly said things like: "I wonder what the weather's going to be like tomorrow." Or, "I hear it's going to be spaghetti and meatballs for lunch in the cafeteria today."

During break Truls and Trym came over to Nilly and Lisa, who were standing by the drinking fountain.

"Well, pip-squeaks," Truls said, towering over them. "What's all this we're hearing about some new powder? Spit it out."

Nilly raised his head and peered up at them, shielding his eyes: "I do believe I can just make out two specimens of Idiotus Colossus. Interesting."

"What did you call us?" Truls asked, moving a step closer. Lisa automatically stepped back, but Nilly didn't budge.

"Idiotus Colossus," he said, smiling. "A dinosaur that lived in the seventeenth century. Very strong and very big. I wouldn't be insulted if I were you."

"Oh?" Truls said, squeezing one eye shut so that he looked like a one-eyed troll. "How strong, huh?"

"Unbelievably strong," Nilly said. "Idiotus Colossus had so many tons of muscles that it was known to have the smallest brain in history in proportion to its body weight."

"Hey!" Trym yelled at Truls. "That dwarf just said 'small brain'!"

"Hey!" Truls yelled at Nilly, grabbing hold of his shirt collar. "You said 'small brain.'"

Nilly sighed. "You guys need to listen more carefully. Idiotus Colossus actually had a brain that's three times the size of your two brains combined. But that's still a small brain in proportion to eighty tons of muscles. Get it? It's simple maths."

Truls and Trym looked at each other uncertainly.

"Enough brain talk," Truls said, letting go of Nilly's collar. "Where's the powder, Mr Tinypants."

Nilly looked around cautiously. "Okay," he whispered. "Since we're practically neighbours, you guys can find out what no one else knows."

Truls and Trym moved in closer to hear what Nilly said.

"Tomorrow, here by the drinking fountain," Nilly

whispered. "Lisa and I are going to tell all the kids at school everything you guys need to know. But only you know this. Okay? Don't tell anyone."

"Cross my heart," Trym said.

Truls looked at Nilly as if there was something he didn't really like, but couldn't quite put his finger on it. And luckily, before he managed to, the bell rang.

That afternoon Lisa, Nilly and Doctor Proctor planned and prepared until sundown. They made a sign to put on the gate so that everyone could find the sale, set up the table with a cash box and change and got the fart powder ready. They filled little plastic bags with one tablespoon of powder from the jar of Doctor Proctor's Totally Normal Fart Powder and decided to sell them for five kroner each. A krone, in case you don't know, is the money used in the very small country of Norway. Although Lisa and Nilly had said that Doctor Proctor should keep the money, the doctor had insisted that they should split what they earned three ways.

"Make sure you don't take it from the wrong jar and put fartonaut powder into the bags instead," Doctor Proctor chuckled.

"No way," said Nilly, who was responsible for putting one teaspoon of the special-formula fartonaut powder into three different envelopes that just needed stamps, since Lisa had already written on them: *To NASA. United States of America. Keep out of reach of children.*

"What are you guys going to do with your share of the money?" Lisa asked.

"I'm going to buy myself a uniform so I can play in the school band," Nilly said.

"I'm going to drive my motorcycle to Paris with the sidecar," Doctor Proctor said. "What about you, Lisa?"

"I'm going to buy an airplane ticket to Sarpsborg and visit Anna," she said. "If we get that much, I mean."

Doctor Proctor laughed. "If not, you can have my third. There's no hurry for my trip to Paris."

"My third too," Nilly said. "I'm sure my mum can sew a band uniform for me."

"Thanks," Lisa said, feeling so happy that her cheeks turned red. Not just because she realised that now she was sure to get enough money to visit Anna, but because she realised that Doctor Proctor and Nilly were so nice to her because they liked her. Lisa liked being liked. Most people do. But she noticed that she especially liked being liked by Nilly and Doctor Proctor.

"What are you going to do in Paris, Doctor?" Nilly asked as he carefully poured powder into one of the bags and then taped it shut.

"Oh, it's a long story," the doctor said, a distant look coming over his eyes. "A long, long story."

"Does it have anything to do with that picture that's hanging in the cellar?" Lisa asked. "The one with you and the girl on the motorcycle in front of the Eiffel Tower?"

"That's right, Lisa," Proctor said.

"Well, let's hear it," Lisa encouraged him.

"Oh, there's not that much to tell," Proctor said. "I had a girlfriend there. Her name was Juliette. We were going to get married."

"Tell us," Lisa whispered eagerly. "Tell us, Doctor Proctor."

"It's just a boring old story, I'm afraid," Doctor Proctor said.

But Lisa didn't back down, and in the end Doctor Proctor gave in. And this is how he told it.

"When I was studying chemistry in Paris many, many years ago, I met Juliette Margarine. She was studying chemistry too, and when we saw each other the first time, there was a . . . uh, 'bang'! She was a brown-eyed beauty and I was . . . well, I was younger than I am now, anyway. And I must have had a certain charm, I guess, because Juliette and I started dating after just a short time. We were inseparable, like two oppositely charged particles in an atom."

"Huh?" Lisa asked.

"Sorry. Like a magnet and a refrigerator door," the professor explained.

"Oh, right," Lisa said.

"Juliette and I were determined to get married when we finished school. But there was one problem. Juliette's father, the Duke of Margarine, was a rich and powerful man who was on the board of the university, and he had totally different plans for Juliette than her marrying a penniless Norwegian without a drop of blue blood in his veins. The day Juliette went to tell her dad that he couldn't stop her from marrying me, she never came back. When I called, they told me that Juliette was sick and couldn't talk to anyone. And especially not me. The next day I got a letter from the board of the university saying that I'd been expelled from the university, because of an experiment that went just a little bit wrong. Well it's not like it was any big deal or anything, just a nitroglycerine mixture that I happened to shake a little too hard, so it exploded and . . . well, caused a bit of damage. But that kind of thing happened all the time and it had been months since it had happened, so I was very surprised. That night a phone call woke me up. It was Juliette. She whispered that she loved me and that she would wait for me. Then she hung up in a hurry. It wasn't until a few days later when the police came to get me that I understood who was behind the whole thing. They gave me a letter that said that I couldn't stay in France anymore, since I wasn't going to school and didn't have a job. Then they drove me to the airport, put me on the first flight back to Norway and said I couldn't come back until I was rich, noble or famous. And since I'm not especially good with money and don't have any aristocratic blood in my veins, I decided to become a famous inventor. Which isn't that easy because so many things have been invented already, but I've been working day and night trying to invent something that is totally and completely new. So that I can go back and find my Juliette."

"Oh," Lisa said when Doctor Proctor was done telling the story. "How romantic."

"You know what?" Nilly asked. "Doctor Proctor's Fartonaut Powder will make you world famous. That's for sure."

"Well we'll see about that," the doctor said.

They heard a grasshopper rubbing its legs together. It was the first one they'd heard that year and it made them realise that summer wasn't far off. Then they glanced up at the moon, which hung pale and almost transparent over the pear tree.

The Big
Fart Powder Sale

NILLY STOOD UP on the drinking fountain so that all the kids could see and hear him.

"Doctor Proctor's Fart Powder will be for sale up at the top of Cannon Avenue. There'll be a sign on the gate!" Nilly yelled, even though it was so quiet that he could have spoken in a totally normal voice.

"We'll start at six p.m. and keep going until seven! No pushing, let the little kids go first and no farting until you've left. Understood?"

"Understood!" they all yelled.

"Any questions?" Nilly asked. He glanced out over the crowd and saw a hand sticking up in the air way in the back. "Yes?"

"Is it dangerous?" a small voice asked.

"Yes," Nilly said seriously. "Unfortunately there is one thing that is dangerous about using this powder."

The faces before him got long, their mouths hanging open.

"You might laugh yourself to death," Nilly said.

A sigh of relief ran through the crowd. The bell rang.

"See you this evening!" Nilly yelled, hopping down from the water fountain. Several people clapped and shouted "Hurray" and a murmur of anticipation rose from the crowd, which slowly dissipated, heading towards the different doors back into the school.

"Do you think anyone's going to come?" Lisa asked Nilly, who was whistling the national anthem to himself in satisfaction.

"You should be asking if there's anyone who *won't* come," Nilly said. "Didn't you see the gleam in their eyes? You might as well go ahead and book that plane ticket to Sarpsborg, Lisa."

"Well all right then," said Lisa, even though deep down she wasn't so sure. But then Lisa was almost never totally sure about anything. That's just the way she was.

"Absolutely positive," Nilly said, raising his hands as if he were playing the trumpet. That's just the way he was.

AFTER SCHOOL LISA and Nilly ran home to complete the final preparations. After dinner they ran back to the doctor's garden where they found

Proctor asleep on the bench. They let him sleep while they attached a sign to the gate. It said:

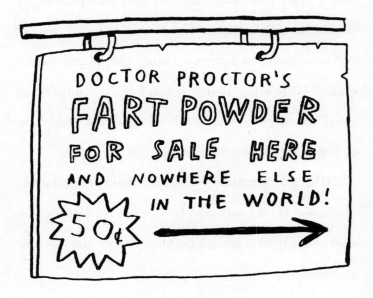

DOCTOR PROCTOR'S
FART POWDER
FOR SALE HERE
AND NOWHERE ELSE
IN THE WORLD!
50¢ ⟶

They took the lids off the shoeboxes and cartons in which the bags of powder were neatly stacked and set them on the picnic table. Then they each sat down in a chair behind the table and started waiting.

"It's ten to six," Lisa stated.

"Excited?" Nilly asked, smiling.

Lisa nodded.

When it was five minutes to six, Lisa told Nilly that it was five minutes to six. The birds were singing in the pear tree. When it was six o'clock, Lisa told Nilly it was six o'clock. And when it was two minutes past six, Lisa looked at her watch for the ninth time since six o'clock.

"Where is everyone?" she asked, worriedly.

"Relax," Nilly said. "We have to give them time to get here." He'd crossed his arms and was dangling his legs contentedly.

"It's five past," Lisa said.

Nilly didn't respond.

At ten past six, they heard Doctor Proctor grunt from the bench. And saw him blinking his eyes. And then suddenly he leaped up, exclaiming, "Good heavens! Did I oversleep?"

"Actually, no," Lisa said. "No one came."

"Yet," Nilly said. "No one has come *yet*. Just wait."

At quarter past six Doctor Proctor sighed almost inaudibly.

At twenty past six, Nilly scratched the back of his head and mumbled something about how kids these days weren't very punctual.

At twenty-five past six, Lisa put her forehead down on the tabletop. "I knew it," she whined.

At six thirty they agreed to pack up.

"Well," Doctor Proctor said, smiling sadly as they put the lid on the last box. "We'll try again another day."

"They're never going to come," Lisa said, sounding choked up. She was on the verge of tears.

"I don't get it," Nilly said, shaking his head.

"Chin up," Proctor said. "I've been inventing things no one wants for years. It's not the end of the world. The main thing is not to give up. Tomorrow I'll invent something that's even more fantastic than Doctor Proctor's Fart Powder."

"But there can't be anything more fantastic than Doctor Proctor's Fart Powder," Nilly said.

"I'm going to go home and go to bed," Lisa whispered, and started walking towards the gate in the front garden with her head down and her arms hanging at her sides.

"Good night," Nilly and Doctor Proctor said.

They sat down on the bench.

"Well," the doctor said.

"Well," Nilly said.

"Maybe I should do a little more work on that time machine I started last year," Proctor said and looked up at the swallows.

"How hard do you think it would be to invent a machine that makes jelly out of air?" Nilly asked and looked up at the swallows.

And that's what they were doing when they heard Lisa's voice from over by the gate.

"You guys . . ." she said.

"Yeah?" the doctor and Nilly said in unison.

"Someone did come," Lisa said.

"Who?"

"You kind of have to come see for yourselves," Lisa said.

Nilly and the doctor got up and went over to the gate.

"Good heavens," Doctor Proctor said, dumbfounded. "What do you say, Nilly?"

But Nilly didn't say anything, because something

extremely rare had happened to Nilly. He was speechless. He couldn't utter a single word. Outside the gate there was a line of children that reached as far as the eye could see. At any rate, as far as you could see on Cannon Avenue.

"Why are you guys so late?" asked the kid at the front of the line, a boy in a cap with the Tottenham football team's logo. "We've been standing here for over half an hour."

Then Nilly finally found his voice again.

"But . . . but why didn't you guys come in?"

"Because it says *here* on the sign, doesn't it?" the boy in the Tottenham hat said. "It says that Doctor Proctor's Fart Powder is for sale *here* and *nowhere else in the world*."

"Yeah, so?" said Nilly, confused.

"And *here* is *here*, right?" the boy said. "And not in *there*." The other kids in line behind him nodded. Then Lisa pulled a marker out of her bag, went over to the sign, drew a line through HERE and wrote THERE in capital letters.

"Then let's get to it!" she yelled so they heard her almost to the end of the line. "No pushing, let the little ones in first and have your money ready!"

THERE WAS STILL a line out there at seven o'clock when Nilly shut the gate, but they were totally out of powder.

"Sold out!" Lisa shouted and said that anyone

who hadn't been able to buy fart powder could come back tomorrow, once Doctor Proctor had made some more. And even though naturally a few people were a little disappointed, they quickly started looking forward to the next day. Because all the way down Cannon Avenue you could already hear the farts banging and the laughter from the kids who had bought the powder.

"Phew," Lisa said, flopping down into a garden chair once everyone was gone.

"Phew," Nilly said.

"You know what?" Doctor Proctor said. "We have to celebrate this. What would you guys say to a little . . ."

"Jelly!" Lisa yelled in delight.

"A three-metre-long jelly!" Nilly yelled, jumping up and down in his chair.

The doctor disappeared, but returned quickly with the longest jelly Nilly and Lisa had ever seen.

"I made this just in case," Proctor said, smiling slyly.

And as the swallows drew strange letters in the evening sky over the pear tree, silence settled over Doctor Proctor's garden. In the end all you could hear was the smacking noise of three mouths devouring a two-and-a-half-metre-long jelly.

Truls and Trym
Blast Off

WHEN LISA WALKED out her front gate the next morning Nilly was standing there with his backpack on.

"Waiting for someone who's going the same way?" Lisa asked.

"Yup," Nilly said.

Then they started walking.

"My mum and dad asked me what was going on at Doctor Proctor's yesterday," Lisa said.

"Did you tell them?" Nilly asked.

"Yeah, of course," Lisa said. "I mean, it's not a secret is it?"

"Nooooo," Nilly said hesitantly. "I just don't usually risk telling my mum about things I think are really fun. Because she almost always decides they're dangerous or naughty or something."

"She may almost always be right, you know," Lisa said.

"Yeah, that's what's so irritating," Nilly said, kicking a rock. "What did your parents say?"

"Dad said it was just fine if I earned some money of my own, then he wouldn't have to earn it for me."

"Oh? So he didn't think it was dangerous?" Nilly asked, a bit skeptical.

"A little farting? Not at all," Lisa said. They walked for a while before Lisa added, "Of course, I didn't tell him about the fartonaut powder."

Nilly nodded. "Probably just as well."

"Anyway I have an idea," Lisa said.

"Well that's definitely good," Nilly said.

"Why?"

"Because you pretty much only ever have good ideas," Nilly said.

"I was thinking that the fart powder doesn't really taste like anything," Lisa said.

"It has absolutely no taste," Nilly said.

"That's what I'm saying. I mean, the farting is fun," Lisa said. "But what if we added a flavour to it, so it tastes good when you eat it too?"

"Like I said," Nilly replied. "Only good ideas. But what kind of flavour?"

"Simple," Lisa said. "What's the best thing you've tasted recently?"

"Simple," Nilly answered. "Doctor Proctor's jelly."

"Exactly! So what we do is add five per cent essence of jelly to the fart powder."

"Brilliant!" Nilly exclaimed.

"Brillll-yant?" they heard a voice say right behind them. "Don't you think that sounds brillll-yant, Trym?"

"It sounds like gobbledygook," said another voice, which may possibly have been even closer.

Nilly and Lisa slowly turned around. They'd been so excited that they'd forgotten to stop and see if the coast was clear before they walked by the house where Trym and Truls lived. And now the two enormous boys were standing there. They were sporting big sneers, each of them chewing on a matchstick, their jaws moving up and down in their enormous, barrel-shaped heads.

"Good morning, boys," Nilly said. "Sorry, but we

have to hurry. Mrs Strobe doesn't like her geniuses to be late to class."

He tried to say it off-handedly and casually, but Lisa could hear in his voice that Nilly wasn't all that confident. He grasped Lisa by the hand and was about to pull her along after him, but Trym was blocking their way.

Truls was leaning against the picket fence, rolling the matchstick from one corner of his mouth to the other. "We didn't get any powder yesterday," he said menacingly.

"You guys must have joined the queue too late," Nilly said, and gulped. "You can try again this afternoon."

Truls laughed. "Did you hear that, Trym? Join the *queue?*"

Trym hurriedly started laughing.

"Listen up, you freckly anteater," Truls said quietly, grabbing Nilly by the collar. "We're not going to be standing in any queue or paying you anything for that fake powder of yours, you catch my drift? We want that powder right here, right now. Or else . . ." The matchstick flipped up and down in the corner of his mouth as he stared at Nilly grimly.

"Or else what?" Nilly whispered.

Truls looked like he was thinking.

"Or else what?" Lisa repeated dully.

"Come on, Truls," Trym said. "Tell them."

"Shut up!" Truls yelled. "Let me concentrate . . ." He concentrated. Then his face lit up. "Yeah, or else we'll smear honey all over you and tie you to the top of this here oak tree. Then the crows will peck you to pieces."

Truls pointed to an oak tree with a trunk that was as big around as four men the size of Lisa's father. And as big around as two men the size of Truls and Trym's father.

They all looked up.

"Oh," Nilly said.

"Oh," Lisa said.

"Uh-oh indeed," Trym said.

Because the oak tree was so tall it looked like the top branches were brushing against the white cloud that was sweeping past up in the sky.

"In that case," Nilly said, "we'll have to see if we can find some kind of a solution. If you could just let me go for a second . . ."

Truls released his grasp and Nilly started rummaging around in his pockets. When he was done with all six of the pockets he had in his trousers, he started on the six in his jacket.

Truls was getting impatient. "Well?" he said.

"I'm almost certain I have a bag here somewhere," Nilly muttered.

"We don't have time for fakers," Truls said. "Trym, get the honey and the rope."

"Wait!" Nilly yelled desperately.

"Let's get the little girl first," Truls said, grabbing Lisa by the arm.

"Here," Nilly said, holding out a bag of greyish powder. "That'll be five kroner."

"Five kroner" Truls grabbed Nilly's wrist, snatched the bag and spit his half-chewed matchstick into the palm of Nilly's hand. "Here, you can have this. Now you can go home and set yourself on fire."

"Ha, ha," Trym laughed.

Truls eyed the bag suspiciously. "What does this say here?" he said. "D-O-C-T-O-R. P-R-O-C – "

"Doctor Proctor's Fart Powder," Lisa said quickly.

"Shut up, I can read!" Truls yelled.

"Well, excuse me," Lisa said, sounding miffed.

"Hmm," Truls said.

"Hmm," Trym said.

"You first," Truls said to Trym.

"No, you first," Trym said to Truls.

"You guys could share," Nilly said.

"Shut up!" Trym yelled, almost as loudly and nastily as Truls just had.

Then they opened the bag and Truls poured exactly half into Trym's hand and half into his own hand. They looked at each other for a second and then swallowed the powder.

"They'll taste better once we add the jelly flavouring – ," Lisa started.

"Shut up!" Truls and Trym yelled, their mouths full of powder.

"Nothing's happening," Truls said, once he'd managed to swallow.

"Seven," Nilly said.

"What the heck?" Trym said.

"Six," Nilly continued. "Five."

Truls turned to look at Lisa. "What's the puny one babbling about?"

But Lisa was offended and showed with her pursed

lips and crossed arms that *she* of all people was not planning on answering.

"Four," Nilly said.

"Truls . . ." Trym said. "I can feel something happening . . . it's like . . . it's like a tickling in my stomach."

Truls scrunched up his forehead and looked down at his own stomach.

"Three," Nilly said. "Two."

"Hey, now I feel it too," Truls said. A big smile spread over his face as Nilly said, "One. Goodbye."

"Huh?" Truls and Trym said. But no one heard them. Because the only thing anyone could hear was the bang that woke up everyone on Cannon Avenue who wasn't awake already. Lisa rubbed the dust, which had blinded her, out of her eyes, but she still couldn't see anyone besides Nilly.

"Where'd they go?" she asked.

Nilly pointed his index finger towards the sky.

Lisa looked at Nilly in disbelief. "You . . . you didn't give them . . . ?"

Nilly nodded.

"The fartonaut powder? You're crazy, Nilly!" Lisa shielded her eyes, staring up into the sky.

"It was them or us," Nilly said, glancing upwards himself.

"They're gone," Lisa said.

"Vanished into thin air," Nilly said.

"I bet it'll be a long time before we see them again," Lisa said.

"Maybe never," Nilly said. "Or, wait a second."

Now that they were getting their hearing back, they were able to hear the rumble of a long fart. And a pitiful voice.

"Help!" the voice was yelling. "Help, we're falling!" It sounded like the long fart and the voice were both coming from the oak tree.

Lisa and Nilly went over to the tree and there,

way up at the top of the tree, they could see the soles of two pairs of shoes. Truls and Trym were dangling by their arms from a branch at the very top of the tree and the long fart was making all the leaves below them shake.

"Mummy!" Truls yelled.

"Daddy!" Trym yelled.

Nilly started laughing, but Lisa grabbed his arm.
"We have to get them down," she said. "They might
get hurt."

"Okay," Nilly said. "Let me just finish laughing
first."

And then he laughed some more. And when Lisa heard that she couldn't help but laugh, too. And all the neighbours who'd been woken up by the bang now opened their windows to peer out and see what caused it. They heard three things: people yelling "Mummy" and "Daddy", people laughing and a flapping noise that reminded them vaguely of . . . but that couldn't be, could it? . . . yes, it was: a real marathon fart.

"If we're going to rescue you guys, you've got to hurry up before the fart ends and do exactly what I say!" Nilly shouted up to Truls and Trym. "Understand?"

"Just get us down!" Truls yelled.

"Grandma! And Auntie!" screamed Trym.

"Lift your legs so your bum is pointing down towards the ground and let go!" Nilly yelled. "Now, right away!"

Truls and Trym were so scared that they just did what Nilly told them. They let go. And then wafted down between the branches, pulling with them a bunch of leaves and acorns and landing rather hard in a heap in front of Lisa and Nilly.

"Well?" Nilly asked, rolling the matchstick from one corner of his mouth to the other. "Do you guys want some more?"

"N-n-no," Trym said.

"All right," Nilly said. "That'll be five kroner."

"Wh-what?" Trym said. "Did you hear that, Truls?"

But Truls hadn't heard. He was lying on his back on the pavement, staring blankly up at the sky, blinking over and over again.

Trym dug down in his trouser pocket and held out the money, which Lisa accepted.

"Well, gentlemen," Nilly said, stuffing the matchstick into his back pocket. "The clock is ticking and unfortunately Lisa and I have to get going."

Nilly and Lisa started running. They made it onto the playground just as the bell rang.

"Hey, Nilly!" It was a boy whose face was vaguely familiar to Nilly. "Cool powder! You wanna come play football at Kålløkka after school today?"

"Nilly!" someone else yelled. "Børre and I are going to come buy more farters tonight. Do you want to come over to Børre's afterwards and play PlayStation or something?"

A girl came over to Lisa. "Some friends are coming over for pizza tonight. Can you come?"

Nilly and Lisa nodded in all directions and ran towards the door to the school.

"Can you believe it, Lisa?" Nilly whispered. "We're popular. You'll see – you'll have a new best friend in no time."

Lisa nodded slowly.

As they filed into the classroom along with everyone else, she tugged Nilly's sleeve:

"Hey, Nilly, I've been thinking."

"Yeah?" Nilly said.

Lisa smiled and looked down.

Nilly wrinkled his forehead. "What is it?"

Lisa opened her mouth and was about to say something. But then it was like she changed her mind and closed her mouth again. And when she opened it again, it was like she was saying something different from what she'd been planning to say originally.

"Well I was thinking that it was strange that you happened to have a bag of fartonaut powder with you," she said. "And especially strange that it said on the bag that it was regular fart powder."

Nilly shrugged.

"You planned that didn't you?" Lisa said. "You filled one of the regular bags with fartonaut powder when we were sitting in Doctor Proctor's garden yesterday. Because you knew Truls and Trym would stop us someday and when they did, you wanted to have a bag with you so you could trick them."

Nilly just smiled in response.

"Isn't that what happened?" Lisa asked.

But just as Nilly was about to respond, they were interrupted by the loud voice of Mrs Strobe saying, "Good morning, my dear children. Take your seats and be completely quiet, please."

And then they all obeyed. Mostly, anyway.

TRULS AND TRYM didn't go to school that day. They stayed home for four good reasons. The first was that the puny devil might have come up with more dirty tricks. The second was that the other kids at school might have heard about what happened and would forget to be scared of Truls and Trym and laugh at them instead. The third was that when it came right down to it, Truls and Trym were two very lazy guys. But the fourth and most important was that they needed help thinking up a way to get revenge. Because no one was better at revenge than their father, Mr Trane. And now their big, fat father was sitting in a big, fat armchair in their big, fat home, scratching his fleshy belly. "Interesting," he said. "So this professor has a powder that can shoot a person right up into the air? Plus another powder that kids are willing to pay money for?"

"Yeah," Truls said.

"Yeah," Trym said.

"Not such dumb inventions," Mr Trane said with an evil sneer as he jabbed a stick into a cage where a frightened guinea pig was trying to get away. "I think I have a plan, boys. A plan that we can all make some money off of."

"Yippee!" cheered Truls.

"Yippee!" yelled Trym. "What's the plan?"

"A little creative borrowing," Mr Trane said.

"Awesome!" cried Truls.

"How do we start?" asked Trym.

"We start, of course . . ." Mr Trane said, grunting as he reached for the phone, "by calling the police."

A Perfect Day?

NILLY AND LISA danced home from school. It was a perfect day. It had started with Truls and Trym eating the fartonaut powder, which blasted them up into the sky. And continued with everyone wanting to be friends with them. Even Mrs Strobe had been in a good mood and when Nilly had given one of his usual unusual answers, she'd laughed so hard she cried, patted him on the head and said that it was remarkable how many strange things he had room for in there. And this afternoon Lisa, Nilly and Doctor Proctor were going to sell even more fart powder, make even more friends and eat even more jelly, and then just wait for Independence Day. So it wasn't so strange that they were dancing. Because what could go wrong?

Nothing, Nilly thought.

Nothing, Lisa thought.

Which is why they didn't give it a second thought when they noticed a police car parked on Cannon Avenue.

"See you this afternoon," Lisa chirped.

"Definitely," Nilly said, practically jumping over his front gate. He ran up the steps, opened the door and was about to go in when he caught sight of a group of people moving through the tall grass towards Doctor Proctor's front gate. There were two

OFFICER
FU MANCHU

men in police uniforms, one of them with a Fu Manchu moustache, the other with a handlebar moustache. They both looked very determined and between them they were holding Doctor Proctor, who was gesticulating and looked very agitated.

"Stop!" Nilly yelled, leaping down from the porch and running over to the fence. "Stop in the name of the law!" The group stopped and turned toward Nilly.

"We *are* the law," Mr Fu Manchu said, "not you."

"What's going on?" Nilly asked. "What do you want with the doctor?"

"He has broken the law,"

OFFICER
HANDLEBAR

Mr Handlebar said. "And we on the police force don't take that kind of thing lightly."

The doctor groaned. "They claim that I sold a deadly powder to children in the neighbourhood here. As if Doctor Proctor's Fart Powder could hurt so much as a fly!"

The two policemen escorted the professor out his gate towards the parked police car. Nilly ran after them.

"Wait!" Nilly yelled. "Who said Doctor Proctor's Fart Powder is dangerous?"

"The father of two boys who were blasted up into the sky by the powder," Mr Fu Manchu said, opening one of the car's rear doors for Doctor Proctor. "He called and said we had to arrest this crazy professor. And of course he's right. Blasting kids up into the sky like that . . . Watch your head there, Doctor."

"Go home and eat your dinner now, Nilly," Doctor Proctor said, ducking his head and taking a seat in the police car. "I'll get this misunderstanding cleared up down at the police station."

But Nilly didn't back down. "Numbskulls! Doctor Proctor didn't give them the powder that sent them up into the oak tree!"

"Numb-what?" Mr Handlebar said gruffly.

"Well then who *did* give them the powder?" Mr Fu Manchu asked.

"I did," Nilly said, standing in front of them resolutely, his hands on his hips.

First the two policemen looked at Nilly, then at each other and then they both started laughing.

"A tiny little guy like you?" Mr Handlebar laughed. "We're supposed to believe that a pip-squeak like you had something to do with such a serious crime?"

"Well," Nilly said, puffing himself up like a frog, "if you'd been paying attention, then those sharp police brains of yours would have noticed that I said the powder had sent them up into an oak tree. You didn't say anything about a tree, so how else would I have known about that?"

"Hmm," Mr Fu Manchu said, raised his police cap and scratched the bald head he had underneath. "You've got a point. So how did you know that?"

"Because I'm telling you what happened!" Nilly hissed. "I'm the one who sold them the powder. And not the normal, harmless powder that Doctor Proctor sells. No sirree, gentlemen . . ."

Nilly took a deep breath and started a very long sentence: "I sold them Doctor Proctor's Fartonaut Powder, even though the doctor himself decided that it should only be sold to NASA, since the powder is a hyper-explosive special formula that can just be consumed in very small doses by people with at least four years of astronaut training, and even then they need to be wearing padding and be

under the supervision of at least two adults!" As Nilly spoke, he got madder and madder and now he was jumping up and down.

"Hmm," Mr Handlebar said. "And who made this . . . uh, fartonaut powder?"

"I did," sighed Doctor Proctor from inside the car.

"But it's my fault that Truls and Trym got hold of it," Nilly said.

"Hmm," Mr Fu Manchu said. "I don't see any way out of this other than to arrest you both. Do you?"

"I agree," Mr Handlebar said.

And that's how both Doctor Proctor and Nilly got arrested on the day that, until that moment, had seemed like it was going to be perfect.

14

Three Fishy Fellas
with a Plan

WHEN LISA'S DAD came home that day, Lisa was
sitting under the apple tree that had no apples.

"I'm so relieved," growled the Commandant,
wiping the sweat off his brow. "We thought the
whole Independence Day celebration was going
to be ruined. You know, Lisa, we've been looking

for the special gunpowder for the Big and Almost World-Famous Royal Salute for several days. We were starting to think they'd forgotten to load it on the ship over in Shanghai. But it turns out it was the first thing they loaded onboard, so it's all the way at the bottom. They're going to bring it ashore tomorrow. Phew, imagine what a catastrophe it would have been if the gunpowder hadn't come!"

Only now did he notice that Lisa was hardly paying attention. She was sitting there under the tree with her head in her hands, looking down-hearted.

"Is there something wrong, pal?" he growled.

"Something terrible happened," Lisa said glumly. "They arrested Nilly and Doctor Proctor. Just because Truls and Trym ate a little fartonaut powder."

"I know," the Commandant said.

"You know? How did you find out?"

"Because the police asked if Nilly and Doctor

Proctor could be kept in the most escape-proof cell in all of northern Europe, apart from Finland. And that's where they are."

"You mean . . . you mean . . ." Lisa began, frightened.

"Yup," her dad said. "They're in the Dungeon of the Dead."

"The Dungeon of the Dead! But Nilly and the professor aren't the least bit dangerous!"

"Well, the police don't agree. Mr Trane explained to the police that the professor is a raving lunatic who'll invent an atom bomb if he isn't locked up immediately."

"Mr Trane? And they believed him?"

"Of course they believed Mr Trane," grumbled the Commandant. "After all he's the one who helped us invent the hardest and most secret material in the world. Which is used in the doors of the most escape-proof cell in the world . . ."

"Yeah, yeah, Dad, I've heard of all that," Lisa sighed. "But what do we do now?"

"Now?" The Commandant noisily sniffed the aroma coming through the open kitchen window. "Eat Wiener schnitzel — at least that's what it smells like. Come on."

AS LISA WENT inside the scent of Wiener schnitzel wafted out over the garden, where a light breeze caught it and carried the scent over Cannon Avenue, down to the fjord, to Akershus Fortress, in over the high stone walls and then past the towers and the black, old-fashioned cannons that were aimed out over the fjord. The guards standing outside the Dungeon of the Dead inhaled the scent without noticing it and the part they hadn't inhaled continued in through the bars to a corridor that led to a stone stairway going deep down, down to a *very* thick and *very* locked iron door.

An exceedingly small amount of schnitzel scent seeped through the keyhole into a room that was shaped like the inside of a cannonball. A bridge ran across the centre of the room and led to another iron door, even thicker and even more locked than the first. And with a keyhole so narrow that only a couple of Wiener schnitzel gas molecules made it into the corridor behind. The darkness in that corridor was penetrated only by laser beams that ran back and forth, up and down. The grid of laser beams was so dense that not even a tiny *Rattus norvegicus* could hope to sneak through without triggering the alarm. And the alarm was connected to the guard-room, where the guard on duty was stationed. And also to the main panel at police headquarters. And also to the command centre for the Norwegian anti-terrorism police. And to the command-command centre for the anti-anti-terrorism police. And I'm sure you can understand, triggering an alarm like that would result in a lot of running and yelling and maybe shooting, and definitely the rather rapid arrest of the little rat or spider that was trying to do something so foolish as to break out of the Dungeon of the Dead.

At the far end of the corridor – and by now there was hardly any scent left – was the final door. It was made out of a material that hardly anyone knows exists, but that is so hard, so ingeniously invented and so secret that the author of this book had to promise the Norwegian government that he wouldn't say anything else about the material in this story. The point – as you may already have surmised – is that the Dungeon of the Dead is absolutely impossible to escape from.

And there, behind that last door, sat Doctor Proctor and Nilly. The walls and ceiling were white, windowless and sort of rounded, so it made them feel like they were sitting inside an egg. Each one was sitting on a bed on either side of the egg cell, which was lit by a single lightbulb that hung from the ceiling. There was a small table between the beds, and a toilet and a sink that were both attached to the wall, and a bookshelf with one single book on it: *King Olav — The People's King*. Nilly had already read it four times. The book had a lot of pictures in it and Nilly had gathered from the text that the best thing about Olav was how good-natured he'd been. But there's a limit to how many times anyone sitting in jail wants to read a book about being good-natured. And not just any old jail, but the most escape-proof jail in all of northern Europe, aside from Finland.

As Nilly read, Doctor Proctor scribbled and sketched something on a scrap of paper he had had in his pocket, scratched his head with the pencil stub, mumbled a few passages in Greek and then scribbled some more. He was so absorbed in his work that he didn't notice Nilly sighing loudly several times, trying to draw his attention to how boring it was for a boy like Nilly to be locked up in a place like the Dungeon of the Dead for as long as it had been. Then all of a sudden Nilly stuck his nose up in the air and sniffed. "Do you smell that, Doctor?"

The doctor stopped and sniffed. "Nonsense. There's nothing to smell."

"For those of us with sensitive noses, there is," Nilly said, concentrating. "Hmm. Could it be French bread? No, further east. Goulash? Further south. Wiener schnitzel? Yes, I really think it must be. Fried in margarine."

Right when Nilly said "margarine" he noticed the doctor's shoulders sink and a sad look come over his face. Nilly hopped up onto the doctor's bed and peeked over his shoulder at what he'd been sketching.

"Nice drawing, boring colours," Nilly said. "What is it?"

"An invention," Doctor Proctor said. "A break-out-of-northern-Europe's-most-escape-proof-jail machine. With probability calculations for its chances of working."

"And what do your calculations tell you?"

"Do you see that number?" the doctor asked, pointing to a number that was underlined twice.

"Yes," Nilly said. "That's a zero."

"That means the probability of escape is zero. We're doomed."

"Don't worry," Nilly said. "They'll come let us out soon. Once they've done a little more investigating and found out that the fart powder is basically harmless."

"I don't think so," the doctor said gloomily, rolling up his scrap paper.

"You don't?" Nilly responded. "Sure they will!"

"I wish they would," the doctor said, tossing his papers at the toilet but missing. "I didn't want to mention this before, but when they were questioning

· 160 ·

me, the police made it pretty clear just what a pickle we're in."

"Why? What did they say, exactly?"

"They said, 'We can't send that little guy named Nilly to jail because he's a kid, but he's looking at at least a year in juvie.'"

"Well, jeez, that wouldn't be so bad," Nilly said. "Maybe that would at least be a place with a band where I could finally do a little trumpet playing. What else did they say?"

Doctor Proctor thought about it, cleared his throat, and continued: "'And you, Doctor, since you're an adult, will be sentenced to up to twelve years behind these walls — or some other walls — and never be allowed to invent anything ever again. Got it?'"

"Yikes," Nilly said. "That's worse."

"A lot worse," Doctor Proctor said. "I can't even bear to think about any part of it — not the twelve years, not the walls and definitely never being allowed to invent anything. I have to escape."

"Hmm," Nilly said. "Where to?"

"To France. I have to find Juliette Margarine. She'll help me, hide me from the police, give me shelter. And Brie. And red wine."

"But how?"

"On my motorcycle, of course. It just needs a little lubrication and then it'll run like, uh, well, like it's been lubricated."

"But how do we get you out of here?"

"I have no clue . . . or, wait a minute!" Doctor Proctor looked like he was lost in thought. "Maybe I made a slight mathematical error. . . ." He leaped up and snatched the crumpled papers off the floor, opened them up, smoothed them out with his hand, let his eyes run up and down the pages, mumbled something and started immediately scribbling and calculating things again. Nilly watched anxiously. Right up until the doctor crumpled the pages up again, threw them over his shoulder and started banging his forehead against the top of the little table.

"It's no use!" he sobbed, covering his head with his arms. "I never make mathematical errors!"

"Hmm," Nilly said, placing his index finger thoughtfully on his chin. "This doesn't look good."

"It looks terrible!" Doctor Proctor yelled. "What are we going to do now?"

"Now?" asked Nilly, who heard the sound of keys rattling and sniffed the air. "It smells like we're going to eat fish cakes."

AFTER DINNER LISA went out into the garden. She needed to think. So she sat down in the grass under the apple tree that had no apples and rested her head in her hands. But the only thoughts that came to her were that the Dungeon of the Dead was completely escape-proof and that Nilly and Doctor Proctor were goners. She burped a Wiener schnitzel burp and mostly felt like crying. So she cried a little and, as usual, crying made her very sleepy, so she yawned a little. And the afternoon sun shone on Lisa and a bird sat on an apple tree branch and sang. But Lisa didn't notice any of it, because she'd fallen asleep. And when something woke her up, it wasn't the birdsong, but voices. The voices were coming from the other side of the fence. There were some people standing in the street talking.

"See that rickety old cellar door there," whispered an adult voice she recognised. "I'm sure it's locked, but you boys won't have any trouble dealing with that."

"Yeah, no problem," said a voice that was even more familiar. "We'll just use a crowbar and pry it open."

"A break-in!" said a third voice and Lisa knew exactly whose it was. "How fun!"

She stood up and peeked cautiously over the fence. And there she saw the backs of three people who were peering cautiously at Doctor Proctor's house.

"Good attitude, boys," whispered Mr Trane's voice.

"And once you're in the doctor's cellar, grab all the fart powder and fartonaut powder you find. Got it?"

"Yes, Dad," Truls said.

"Yes, Dad," Trym said.

"And then, boys, you can sell the fart powder to the kids at school."

Suddenly they turned around, but Lisa was faster and ducked.

"What about the fartonaut powder, Dad?" Truls asked.

"Heh, heh," Mr Trane laughed. "I've already talked to someone in the U.S., in Houston, who's very interested in an invention that can send people right into space without having to build a rocket."

"Who? Who did you talk to, Dad," Trym asked.

"NASA, you idiot," Mr Trane said. "Once we get our hands on the powder, I'm going straight down to the patent office to patent the fartonaut powder. And then, too bad, mister nitwit professor, I'll be the only one who can sell the powder. I'm going to be a millionaire, boys!"

"Aren't you already a millionaire, Dad?"

"Well, sure. But with a few more million, I can buy another Hummer. And an indoor swimming pool. What do you say to that?"

"Oh, yeah, Dad!" Truls and Trym shouted in unison.

"Okay," their father said. "Now we know how it's going to go down. We'll get the crowbar and ski masks and then tomorrow night, we strike! Heh, heh, heh."

Lisa sat motionless, listening as she heard Mr Trane's laughter and all of their footsteps fade into the distance. Then she leaped up and ran inside.

"Dad, Dad!" she shouted.

"What is it, Lisa?" rumbled the Commandant, who was lying on the sofa reading the paper.

She hurriedly told her dad about how she'd been woken up from her sleep and had overhead the Trane family's plans. But as she was talking, a smile spread across the Commandant's face.

"What is it?" she cried when she was done. "Don't you believe me?"

"You never lie, Lisa dear," the Commandant said, chuckling. "But don't you see that you just dreamed it all while you were sleeping, that you weren't actually awake? Mr Trane and his family, breaking into the doctor's house and stealing his invention?" The Commandant laughed so hard he shook. "Can you imagine?"

Lisa slowly realised that if even her own father didn't believe her, who would? Who could help her? And the answer was just as clear: no one. No one except herself.

The sun had just set and tomorrow, Doctor Proctor's Fart Powder would be in the hands of those three fishy fellas. And Lisa was the only one who knew it.

The Dungeon
of the Dead

THAT NIGHT A sound woke Nilly up. He pushed himself up and leaned on his elbow. In the darkness he could hear Doctor Proctor snoring from the other bed. But Nilly knew that wasn't the sound that had woken him up. For a second he wondered if maybe it wasn't the rumbling from his own stomach, because they hadn't had anything to eat since those measly fish balls. But he dismissed that thought. Because Nilly had the distinct sense that he and Doctor Proctor were no longer alone in the cell. . . .

He stared into the darkness.

And all he saw was darkness.

But in the sole strip of light that filtered in through the keyhole, he suddenly saw something. A glimpse of white and fairly sharp teeth. Then they were gone again.

"Hey there!" Nilly yelled, throwing off his wool blanket, jumping off the bed, and running over to the door, where he flipped on the light switch.

Doctor Proctor's snoring had stopped and when Nilly turned around he saw the professor standing on his bed in just his underwear, as white in the face as he was on the rest of his body and pointing at the animal that was now visible.

"It's — it's — it's a . . ." the professor stammered.

"I see what it is," Nilly said.

"I – I – I'm scared to death of – of – of . . ." said the doctor.

"Of that animal there?" Nilly asked.

The doctor nodded, pressing his quaking body against the wall. "Look at the tee-tee-teeth on that beast."

"Beast?" Nilly said, squatting down in front of the animal. "This is a *Rattus norvegicus*, Doctor. A friendly, little *Rattus norvegicus* who's smiling. Sure, it's mentioned in a footnote in *Animals You Wish Didn't Exist* by W. M. Poschi, but that's just because it spreads the Black Death and other harmless diseases."

SNIFF
SNIFF

RATTUS NORVEGICUS

The rat blinked at Nilly with brown rat eyes.

"I can't help it," Doctor Proctor said. "Rats give me the shi-shi-shivers. Where did it come from? How did it get in here?"

"Good question," Nilly said, scratching his head and looking around. "Tell me, Doctor, are you thinking what I'm thinking?"

Doctor Proctor stared at Nilly. "I – I – I think so."

"And what are we thinking?"

"We're thinking," said the doctor, totally forgetting to be afraid and hopping down onto the floor and pulling on his professor coat, "that if it's possible to get into a place, it must be possible to get back out of the same place."

"Exactly," Nilly said, holding out a finger that the little rat sniffed out of curiosity. "So I recommend that we pay close attention to our rat friend when he heads home."

The Great Escape

NILLY'S SISTER ANSWERED the door when Lisa rang the doorbell of the yellow house the next morning. Eva gazed at Lisa with her narrow, kind-of-evil eyes, which glowed just as angrily as the two new spots she had on her face and said in a taunting, squeaky voice, "Nilly's not here, Flatu-Lisa."

"I know," Lisa said. "He's in jail."

Eva's eyes got big. "In jail?"

"Yup. In the Dungeon of the Dead."

"Mum!" Eva yelled over her shoulder. "Nilly's in jail!"

They heard someone rummage around, drop several things, fall over and maybe swear a little.

"Haven't you wondered why you haven't seen him for twenty-four hours?" Lisa asked.

Eva shrugged. "It's not easy to spot something so tiny, so I don't think it's that strange if I don't see him for a few days, you know? It's kind of a nice break."

"Well anyway," Lisa said, "prisoners in the Dungeon of the Dead are only allowed to receive visits from people in their immediate family, so I was wondering if you could give him this letter." She held out an envelope.

"We'll have to see," Eva said, snatching the letter. "If we have time."

NILLY AND DOCTOR Proctor were both lying on the floor of the cell, snoring and sleeping, when they were shaken awake by a member of the Royal Guard serving as a prison attendant in a black uniform and hat with a big, silly tassel on it.

"Huh? We must have fallen asleep watching the rat," Nilly said, rubbing his eyes.

"Visitor for prisoner number 000002," the guard said gruffly.

"Is that me?" Nilly asked, still half-asleep. "Or is that him?"

"It's you," the guard said. "He's prisoner number 000001."

Nilly looked around and said, "Where? Where?"

"That guy, right there," the guard said, irritated, pointing at the professor, who was still snoring softly.

"No, not him!" Nilly shouted. "The rat! Did a rat run out the doorway when you came in?"

"Not that I saw," the guard said. "Look, do you want your visitor or not?"

Nilly followed the guard through all the thick, but now open doors, down the corridor where the laser beams had been turned off, over the bridge, up the stairs, through the open door with the metal bars, and into the visiting room. And there was Eva, sitting in a chair chewing gum.

"Hi," Nilly said, surprised, and smiled at his sister. "How nice that you wanted to come visit me."

"As if," Eva said. "I didn't want to. Mum sent me. She didn't feel like she was quite up to a prison visit herself. I brought you a letter. From that weird neighbour girl."

"Lisa?" Nilly said, lighting up and taking the envelope. He could tell right away that it had been opened. "Well, what did she say?" he asked bitterly.

"How should I know?" Eva asked innocently.

Nilly read the letter silently and put it in his pocket.

"What's NASA?" Eva asked.

"Anything else new?" Nilly asked.

Eva snorted and stood up. "I've got to go to school. Have a nice day in jail."

Once Nilly was safely back under lock and lock and lock and key with the professor, he passed him the letter. Doctor Proctor read aloud:

Bad news. The Trane family is going to break into the professor's cellar tonight, steal the fartonaut powder, patent it and sell the invention to NASA. We have to do something. Lisa

"This is hopeless," the professor blurted out. "They're going to rob me! Steal my invention."

"Lisa's right," Nilly said. "We have to do something. We have to get out of here."

"But how?" the professor asked. "The rat is gone. We don't know how it got out. "

"Well," Nilly said, "give me the letter. We'll flush it down the toilet so no one finds out that Lisa's working with us. Otherwise they'll put her in jail too."

Nilly crumpled up the letter, tossed it into the toilet and flushed. The toilet made a long, loud gurgling sound, the paper disappeared and then the toilet bowl filled back up with water. Nilly stood there thoughtfully watching the ripples in the bowl where the paper had just been and scratching his scalp through his red hair. And what he was thinking about was how the letter was being carried down through the pipes by the water. Down and down. Until it splashed down into a bigger sewer pipe somewhere way down below them. A sewer pipe that must surely stink and be teeming with . . .

"You know what?" Nilly said. "I think I just figured out where our rat friend went."

"Really?" the professor said.

Nilly pointed down into the toilet.

"It swam up here through the pipes from the sewer. And went back out the same way."

"Pyew!" the professor said, holding his nose.

"Maybe," Nilly said. "But from the sewer pipe, the water keeps going. And going. All the way until it gets to the ocean. Or maybe to a treatment plant. And along the way there are ladders up to the street above, to manhole covers that lead right out onto the streets of Oslo. Do you get where I'm going with this, Professor?"

The professor, who clearly got where Nilly was going, stared at him in disbelief. "You must be crazy!" he exclaimed.

"Not crazy," Nilly laughed. "Just very smart. And

very, very small. We can only hope that I'm small enough."

"You can't!" Doctor Proctor said. "You mustn't!"

"I can, I must and I will," Nilly said.

"The guards look in here all the time – they'll notice that you're gone."

"We'll wait until early evening," Nilly said. "Then we act like we're going to bed early and turn off the light. And then in the dead of night . . ."

THE SUN DRIFTED across the sky and its rays fell on an Oslo that had started preparing for Independence Day, which was only two days away. People were cleaning up their houses and planting flowers in window boxes, ironing flags and the aprons that went with their national costumes, reviewing traditional eggnog recipes and humming the national anthem. And as the sun began to descend towards Ullern

Ridge at the western edge of the city, the men at the wharf carried the last of the crates off the ship from Shanghai.

The rays that penetrated between the planks of the wharf reflected off some seashells. And not just the kinds of shells that are attached to wharf pilings and the rocks that are only visible at low tide. But shells that moved. Shells that were black and attached to the back of something slithering out of the dark opening of a sewer pipe. Shells on the back of something that hadn't eaten anything since the leathery meat on that thirty-five-year-old Mongolian water vole a few days ago . . .

The creature slides through the water. It hears the wharf planks creaking. Sees the soles of a pair of boots. *Food.* It's a man carrying a wooden crate. The creature quickly twists its way up around one of the wharf pilings, up into the blinding sunlight and rises, swaying above the poor guy, and it hears the footsteps on the wharf stop. The creature opens its jaw, the sun shines on its gruesome fangs and it hears a scream. *Yes, yes, this is how food sounds*, it thinks.

The creature gets ready for a bulky mouthful. But the afternoon sun is so low and still so glaring and the creature hasn't seen any light in days. So it strikes blindly, grabs hold of something, seizes it and swiftly vanishes into the water. And then into the sewer pipe. *Food!* The creature can already feel its digestive juices starting to flow from glands throughout its body as it swims its way back into the Oslo sewer system. And then, deep in the sewers, in a strip of light that falls from a little hole for runoff water on a manhole cover in a street way up above, it stops to really enjoy its meal. But . . . what is this? Wood taste? The creature spits the food out. And it isn't food at all. It's a wooden crate. The creature fumes with rage. Blast it! Doggonit! How aggravating!

But then the creature hears something. An echo

from a squeak within the sewer system. A rat squeak? *Rattus norvegicus. Food!* And *whoosh*, the starving creature is swallowed up by the darkness of the sewer, on the hunt again. Leaving the wooden crate floating there, bobbing up and down in the sewer water. And in the strip of light from the manhole cover, one can read the following printed on the lid in red letters: CAUTION! HIGHLY EXPLOSIVE SPECIAL GUNPOWDER FROM SHANGHAI FOR THE BIG AND ALMOST WORLD-FAMOUS ROYAL SALUTE AT AKERSHUS FORTRESS.

THE SUN SANK even further towards Ullern Ridge and started to slip behind it. The last rays cast long, white fingers over the landscape, as if the sun were desperately trying to hang on. And the rays reached all the way to Cannon Avenue. But it lost its hold and then the sun was gone.

It was evening. Truls and Trym stood in one of their three garages on Cannon Avenue, watching

Mr Trane, who had pulled a black crowbar out of the toolbox in his black Hummer. He had already given each of them a ski mask, which would cover their whole heads and faces apart from their eyes and mouth, so they could see and breathe and talk a little. Nice when it's really cold out. Or when you're going to commit a robbery. Because even if someone sees you during the robbery, they're guaranteed not to recognise you afterwards. Unless you're still wearing the ski mask of course.

"Like so," Mr Trane demonstrated, sliding the crowbar in along the edge of a door. "And so and then so."

"Like this," Truls and Trym repeated through their ski masks. "And this and then this."

They repeated and repeated and practised and practised the break-in. But it took some time, because Truls and Trym weren't the smartest boys in the world. And not just not the smartest boys in the world, actually. They were also not the smartest boys in Norway, or the smartest boys in Oslo, or even the smartest boys on Cannon Avenue. Because at that very moment the smartest boy on Cannon Avenue was sitting on a bed in the Dungeon of the Dead, feeling nervous. More nervous than he'd ever been before. Yes, so nervous that he bordered on being scared. And scared was something that Nilly, prisoner number 000002, very rarely was.

"What are you doing?" he asked Doctor Proctor, who'd taken off his professor's coat, turned the pockets inside out and was now carefully brushing the pocket lining over one of his scraps of paper.

"I was thinking," the professor said. "It's going to be awfully dark when you get down there. And you don't have a torch. Then I remembered that there is always residue in my pockets from some of the various powders I've invented. And voilà . . ."

Nilly came over and looked down at the sheet of

paper, where there was a fine layer of light-green powder.

"I've seen that before," Nilly said. "That's Doctor Proctor's Light-Green Powder. You had it in a jar in your cellar. You said it was a phosphorescent powder that makes you glow. And that it was a rather unsuccessful invention."

"Maybe it isn't so unsuccessful after all," the professor said, carefully folding the piece of paper in half so that all the powder slid into the fold. "Open wide!"

With Nilly's mouth open as wide as it would go, the professor poured the powder into the small opening.

"It'll take a little while before it starts working," the professor said. "And meanwhile . . ." He intensely brushed out the other coat pocket over the sheet of paper.

"Is that what I think it is?" Nilly asked when he

spotted the small, light-blue grains sitting on the professor's mathematical calculations.

"Yup," the professor said. "It's fartonaut powder. Too bad I don't have more here."

"But what do I do with it?"

"The exits to the sewer system are blocked by manhole covers," the professor said. "And they're heavy and hard to move. If you need to get out, you should – "

"Fart one of them up into the sky!" cried the smartest boy on Cannon Avenue.

The professor nodded and poured the fartonaut powder into the envelope that Lisa's letter had come in. "But there's only enough here for one good fart, so don't waste it."

"I won't," Nilly said, folding up the envelope and stuffing it into his trouser pocket.

The professor studied him for a moment. "Your face is green. Are you feeling sick?"

"No," Nilly said, surprised. "Just a little . . . uh, nervous."

"Good, then it's the glowing powder starting to work. Quick, we'd better act now before it stops working."

The professor went over to the door and put his finger on the light switch. He hesitated.

"Come on," Nilly said.

The professor sighed and turned off the light and it got pretty dark. But not completely dark. Because in front of him Nilly could see a glimmering green light, he just couldn't see where it was coming from. Until he looked down at himself.

"Hey!" he yelled. "You can see right through me! I can see my own skeleton!"

"And you're glowing," the professor said. "You're your own torch. Now hurry up!"

Nilly crawled up onto the rim of the toilet and hopped down into the water, making a splash.

"Brr," he said.

"Ready?" the professor asked, looking down at the tiny little, and now phosphorescent, boy who was treading water in the toilet.

"Ready," Nilly said.

"Take a deep breath and hold it," the professor said.

"Roger!" Nilly said, taking a breath and pinching his nose.

And with that, the professor flushed. The toilet gurgled and spluttered and sloshed. And then it turned into a steady rushing noise and the professor peered into the toilet and Nilly wasn't there anymore.

Life in the Sewers

NILLY WAS IN a free fall. He had once tried the waterslide at some water park or other, but this was totally different. His body whooshed like a torpedo towards the centre of the earth until a bend in the pipe flung him to the left. And then to the right. And then straight down again. He felt like a cowboy riding a wild horse of water, and he couldn't help himself — he had to yell, "Yee ha!"

The pipes were exactly big enough with exactly enough water to soften all the falls and turns. He was carried further and further down and, although it was getting both darker and colder, he was having so much fun and things were glowing so green around him that he wasn't thinking about being wet or freezing cold. And he realised why that rat in their cell had swum and scrambled all the way up into their toilet: this was the roller-coaster ride of a lifetime!

It felt like such an adrenaline rush in his stomach every time the pipes turned and Nilly plunged into a new free fall that he hoped the ride would never end. But it did have to, of course. And it did. Rather suddenly too. The walls of the narrow pipe disappeared and he was stretched out in the air as flat as a pancake and saw something black approaching with alarming speed. Then the black thing hit him.

Or to be more precise, Nilly hit the black thing. No one has ever witnessed an uglier belly flop in the Oslo sewer system. Brown, slimy goo sloshed up against the walls. And, boy, did it sting! Nilly felt like he was lying facedown in a frying pan.

He stood up and discovered that the water only came up to his waist. He looked around. Besides the glimmering green light coming from him, it was pitch-black. And once the sloshing had subsided, it was completely quiet too. But, yuck, it stank! It smelled so bad that the author advises you to do the same thing Nilly realised he had to do: Stop thinking about it.

What was I thinking about? Nilly wondered, since he wasn't thinking about the smell anymore. *Right, that I need to find a manhole cover.* And with that Nilly started wading through the sewer system looking for a way out.

Unfortunately it's not as easy as you might think to find a manhole cover in a sewer system after the sun has set. The reason being that the sun is no longer shining through the manhole covers' small holes that are designed to let water in from the street. And although Nilly was glowing the light didn't reach far enough to illuminate the shafts above him. But he didn't give up.

AFTER NILLY HAD waded for a long time and quite some distance, he heard a hissing sound. And he thought the hissing sound must be coming from a manhole cover. Because obviously hissing sounds don't come from the sewer. *Who on earth would be hissing down here?* he thought.

But he wasn't totally sure and noticed that as he approached the location where he thought the sound had come from, his heart beat faster. A lot faster . . .

And as he rounded a corner, he froze and stood still. Completely still. Actually stiller than he'd ever stood before.

Because he thought he'd seen something.

Something that had gleamed at the very edge of the circle of green light. A row of much too white, much too sharp and, most of all, much too big teeth. Because teeth that big and that sharp should not be down in the Oslo sewer system. They should only be found in the Amazon River and thereabouts. Or in a dreadful picture on page 121 of *Animals You Wish Didn't Exist*. More specifically, in the mouth of the world's largest and most feared constrictor. The anaconda.

It had been a long time since Nilly had read the anaconda chapter in the thick, old book from his grandfather, but now he could clearly picture every single dusty word. And Nilly realised that he was in trouble. First of all, because he was standing up to his waist in what, according to his grandfather's book, was the anaconda's favourite element: water. Not very clean water, but water all the same. Secondly, because Nilly was probably the most visible thing in the Oslo sewer world right about now: a transparent, glowing, green boy. And thirdly, because even if he hadn't been a glowing larva, there still wouldn't have been anywhere to hide.

So he kept standing there. And there was that hissing noise again. And there were those teeth gleaming in the light again. And they were attached to the biggest mouth he'd ever seen. On each side of the mouth, an evil anaconda eye was staring at him, and in the middle of the mouth, a split red anaconda tongue was vibrating. And Nilly had to admit that even the dreadful picture on page 121 didn't do

the creature justice. Because this was much, much worse and way creepier. The mouth came towards him relentlessly.

AND NOW AS Nilly is about to be eaten, maybe you hope that something will happen at the last minute, something completely unlikely, the kind of thing that never happens anywhere besides in stories just as the hero is about to meet his demise. But nothing like that happened. All that happened was that Nilly slid right down the gullet of the giant snake, glowing all the way. And only two days before Independence Day.

A FULL MOON hid behind a cloud over Cannon Avenue as if it didn't dare watch. Truls and Trym stood by the fence to Doctor Proctor's garden.

"Breaking in is fun," Truls whispered.

"Breaking in is fun," Trym whispered.

But even though they were whispering they still

made too much noise. The moon emerged from the clouds and cast shadows that ran across the over-grown garden like big men in hats and capes.

"Maybe I should stand watch out here while you go in and get the fart powder?" Truls suggested.

"Shut up," Trym said, staring at the crooked wooden house in front of them, which didn't have any lights on. The house that was so small in the daylight seemed enormous in the dark.

"Are you a tiny bit scared?" Truls asked.

"Nope," Trym said. "You?"

"No way. Just wondering if you were."

"Come on," Trym said, and climbed over the fence. When they were on the inside, they stood still and listened. But all they could hear were a couple of grasshoppers that had lost track of the time and the wind rustling in the pear tree and making the walls of the house creak and groan like an old man telling dusty old ghost stories.

They waded through the grass towards the house. Truls could hear his own heartbeat. And maybe Trym's too. When they got to the cellar door, Trym held the crowbar up.

"Wait!" Truls whispered. "Check if it's locked first."

"You idiot," Trym hissed. "You don't think he'd be so stupid that he would keep a fortune's worth of fart powder in an unlocked cellar, do you?"

"Who knows?"

"You want to bet on it?"

"I'll bet you a bag of fart powder."

"Okay."

Truls pulled down on the door handle and tugged. And do you know what? It turned out that the door was actually . . . was actually . . . *locked*! What did you think? That someone would be so stupid that he would keep a fortune's worth of fart powder in an unlocked cellar?

"Darn it," Truls said.

"Hurray," said Trym, pressing the tip of the crowbar inbetween the door and the frame and pushing on the other end.

It creaked a little. It creaked a little more.

"Wait!" Truls said.

"Not again," Trym groaned.

"Look at the window."

Truls looked at the window. And then eased up on the crowbar.

"Broken," he said. "Must have been some pranksters throwing rocks."

"Or some rotten sneaky thieves who beat us to it."

They climbed in through the window and turned on their torches.

The cones of light from their torches slid over all kinds of strange equipment, test tubes, barrels, drums, tubes, glass containers and an old motorcycle with a sidecar. And stopped on two enormous jars.

"The powder!" Truls whispered.

They moved closer and shone the light on the labels. The writing on them was the kind of swoopy lettering Mrs Strobe had tried to teach them, but that neither Truls nor Trym had really got the hang of.

"*Doctor Proctor's Totally Normal Fart Powder*," Truls read one with difficulty.

"*Fartonaut Powder*," Trym read the other one. "*Keep out of reach of children.*"

"Heh, heh," Truls laughed.

"Ho, ho," Trym laughed. "This'll make Dad happy."

"And then we'll get a swimming pool. Come on, bro."

With that they each grabbed a jar and snuck back out the same way they'd come in. And only the moon saw them as it timidly peeked out from between the hurrying clouds.

And maybe one person in the red house across the street. At any rate, the curtains in one of the windows on the first floor moved a little.

The Even Greater
Escape

THE SUN CAME up over Oslo and Akershus
Fortress. And there was a great commotion there.

"What do you mean," growled the Commandant,
"the gunpowder from Shanghai is *missing*?"

"It disappeared while we were unloading it onto
the wharf yesterday afternoon, sir," said the steadfast,

but obviously nervous, guardsman in front of him.

"Disappeared? How is that possible?"

"The longshoreman swears it was eaten by a big snake, sir."

The Commandant's growl made the window-panes in his office rattle. "Are you trying to convince me that some snake ate the whole crate of gunpowder?"

"No, sir. The longshoreman is trying to convince me of what I'm trying to convince you, sir."

The Commandant's face was now so red and his stomach so inflated that the guardsman was afraid he might explode at any moment. "Excuses! That butterfingers dropped the crate in the water! Do you know what this means, my dear guardsman?"

And the guardsman knew what it meant. It meant that for the first time in over a hundred years, there wouldn't be any Royal Salute. People from Strømstad, just across the border in Sweden, to Poland, and yes, even all the way to Madagascar, would scoff at their little country way up north, make fun of them and call them things that rhyme with Norway. Gorway and borway and sporway and things that might not sound so bad in English, but that could mean really preposterous things in Madagascarian.

"What do we do now?" asked the guardsman.

And like a big red balloon that suddenly popped, the Commandant sunk down into his chair, thumping his forehead against his desk, and then stopped moving. He tried to say something, but his lips were squashed against the top of the desk so it was impossible to understand him.

"Um, what?" asked the guardsman.

The Commandant raised his head off the desk. "I said, I don't know."

BUT THE SUN kept shining and smiling as if nothing had happened. And it really shouldn't have on a day like this. Because let's review the situation, dear reader. The Commandant's gunpowder is missing. Nilly has been eaten. Doctor Proctor is in jail. And his powder has been stolen by the evil Trane family.

So why does Lisa seem both happy and unconcerned as she plays her clarinet and marches down the streets of the city in the Dølgen School Marching Band at the crack of dawn on the day before Independence Day? Could she have forgotten all of their problems? Is she maybe not who we thought she was? Does she actually not care about her friends at all? Or does she know something we don't?

Perhaps, but we also know something she doesn't know. We know that Nilly was eaten by an anaconda. And the only other one, aside from us and the snake, who knows that is Nilly himself.

I'VE BEEN EATEN by an anaconda, Nilly thought as he sat there in the darkness inside a snake's body that was moving and slithering and dripping from the ceiling and walls. He was still sore from having been kneaded through the snake's jaws and throat, but there was more room in here and he was still more or less in one piece. But, of course, that was just a matter of time. Because he knew from page 121 in *Animals You Wish Didn't Exist* that the stuff dripping on him was a highly corrosive blend of digestive juices. And that in time it would dissolve Nilly's body into its individual components. As it had done to the poor thing that had owned the metal collar Nilly had found when he'd ended up in here the night before.

Nilly'd just had time to read the name engraved on the collar before his phosphorescent powder had stopped working: *Attila*. That was all that was left of the poor thing. The digestive juices had already started eating away at the soles of Nilly's shoes and the scent of burning rubber stung his nostrils. There was little doubt that he was facing a slow and rather gruesome death. There was also little doubt that his hopes that the constrictor would sneeze or hiccup him back out were dwindling rapidly. But there was no doubt that he had to think of something, and he had to do it in a flash.

So Nilly thought of something.

He pulled the envelope of fartonaut powder out of his pocket.

THE CONSTRICTOR ANNA Conda woke up suddenly. It had been dreaming the same dream it always dreamed. That it was swimming with its mother in the delightfully warm waters of the Amazon River among the piranhas, crocodiles, poisonous snakes, and other good friends, and was as happy as a hippo. And that one night it was captured, snatched out of the water and shipped to a freezing-cold country, where it had ended up in a pet store. And that one day a fat little boy had come in with his father, who had yelled at the shop owner and shown her the bite marks on his fat little boy's hand. Then the little boy had discovered the snake. His face had lit up and he had shoved his dad, pointed and yelled: "Anna Conda!" and then that was its name. Even though Anna Conda was a girl's name and he was a boy! Or that's what he thought, anyway.

Anna Conda had been put in a cage in Hovseter and had been fed some pasty white, round, slippery balls that tasted like fish, while the little boy poked it in the side with sticks. And even though this had all happened more than thirty years ago, Anna Conda would still wake up from this awful nightmare and would have been drenched in sweat if constrictors could sweat. And then it sighed in relief, because it wasn't in the apartment in Hovseter, but in the delightfully warm sewer pipes beneath downtown Oslo.

What had happened was that one night the little boy had forgotten to lock the cage and so Anna Conda had managed to escape through the open bedroom window, down along the downspout to the street, where after a great deal of searching and a couple of hysterical women's screams, it had found a loose manhole cover. That first night in the Oslo Municipal Sewer and Drainage System, it had lain curled up in a corner scared to death. But that fear had quickly passed. And by the next day, it had started doing what anacondas do: squeezing things very tightly and then eating them. Because there were lots of *Rattus norvegicus*, bats and regular old mice down there. It wasn't quite the Amazon, perhaps, but it wasn't that bad either. Just the other day it had even come across a genuine Mongolian water vole.

Now that Anna Conda had got so big, it had started easing up on constricting the food first — it just swallowed it, which was so much easier. It was pretty sure it remembered its mother saying that it wasn't good table manners to swallow food without properly squeezing it first, but there wasn't anyone down here to notice. So Anna Conda had just swallowed the tiny, glowing piece of meat with the red hair. But now it had the feeling that that might not have been such a good idea. Because the reason it had woken up was that it suspected something had exploded somewhere inside it and that a massive burp was on its way and wanted out. And Anna Conda suspected that the food was planning to go the same way. So Anna Conda clenched its jaws shut as it felt its long body inflate. And inflate. But it didn't give up; it clenched its jaws harder. Its body began to resemble an enormous sausage-shaped balloon and it was still swelling. But Anna Conda didn't give up; *what's eaten is eaten* he thought. It was so inflated now that its snaky black scales were squished against the sides of the sewer pipe. Its jaws ached. Soon it wouldn't be able to take anymore. And the pressure from within was only getting worse.

Soon it wouldn't . . .

It wouldn't . . .

Wouldn't!

Anna Conda's mouth popped open and out came a burp. We're not just talking about a regular burp, but a thunderclap of a burp that caused all of southwestern Oslo to shake in its foundations. And, just like when you stop pinching together the end of a sausage-shaped balloon, Anna Conda took off like a rocket through the Oslo sewer system. *Vroom!* Just like a cannonball being shot out of a cannon. The speed increased and so when it was shot out of the sewer pipe under the wharf a few nanoseconds later, it kept going quite a long way out over the fjord before it turned and headed straight up into the air. And exactly like a runaway balloon it made sudden, unpredictable turns all over the place, accompanied by a flapping, farting sound.

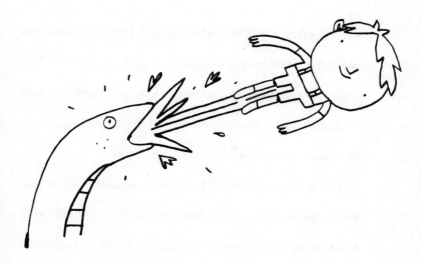

Until it was completely deflated and it landed like a moth-eaten lion pelt in a spruce tree somewhere out on the Nesodden Peninsula.

Nilly, however, was lying on his back, floating in the sewer water like a piece of poop, as he stared up at the ceiling and laughed. His laughter echoed through the network of sewer pipes. He was free! He'd been shot out of the anaconda's jaws like a projectile about one minute after he'd swallowed the fartonaut powder. Who would have thought it would feel so liberating to be in a sewer!

But after a while Nilly stopped laughing. Because actually, all of his problems were far from solved. The snake would soon find its way back into the sewer and he really didn't want to be there when that happened. And how was he going to not be there?

He had to get out. He looked around. There was not a single exit sign to be seen. Just a wooden crate bobbing up and down in the water in the semi-darkness. He clambered up onto it and paddled inwards. Or outwards. He wasn't sure which way. And after he'd paddled around various turns and corners for twenty minutes, he still didn't know where he was or how he was going to find an exit. He stopped paddling. And as he sat there listening to the silence, he thought he heard a faint sound. No, he wasn't imagining it, it *was* a sound. And it was getting louder. A terrible sound. The sound of an explosion, a plane crash and an avalanche. A sound that sends shivers down your spine and sends the devil packing. And Nilly knew that that sound could only be one thing: the Dølgen School Marching Band.

Nilly paddled as fast as he could towards the sound, went around two corners and sure enough he saw a beam of sunlight coming down from something that could only be a shaft leading up to the surface. Nilly paddled over to a metal ladder that was bolted to the side of the shaft and looked up. The ladder led up to where the light was coming from, somewhere way up above him. And, there, up at the top he saw the bottom of a manhole cover. Nilly hopped off the wooden crate and climbed up as fast as he could. When he was halfway up he glanced down, causing his heart to skip a beat and making him immediately promise himself that he wouldn't do that again. Sometimes it's just better not to know how high up you are.

When Nilly had made it all the way to the top and could hear the sound of the Dølgen School Marching Band moving away, he put his shoulder against the manhole cover and pushed as hard as he could. Then he tried one more time. And again. But unfortunately what Doctor Proctor had said was true: the manhole covers in this city would not budge. And there wasn't a single grain of fartonaut powder left for him to blast the iron cover off with.

Nilly shouted as loud as he could: "Help! Help!"

The sound of the most hideous marching band music in the Northern Hemisphere was almost gone now and Nilly's shouts were drowned out by the cars that had started driving on the street above him.

"Help! Help!" Nilly shouted. "There's an anaconda living down here and it's on its way home for lunch!"

Nilly knew probably no one would believe that, but what did it matter since no one could hear him anyway?

Nilly held on until his arms ached and he shouted until he was so hoarse that only a low rasping came from his throat. Resigned, he climbed back down and lay on the crate, exhausted. Then he sat up and started listening for the sound of a snake hissing. And while he was sitting like that, he happened to see a ray of light from the manhole cover shine on some deep holes punched through the lid of the crate he was sitting on. Holes left by large and rather sharp fangs. And some red letters that were printed on the lid:

CAUTION! HIGHLY EXPLOSIVE SPECIAL GUNPOWDER FROM SHANGHAI FOR THE BIG AND ALMOST WORLD-FAMOUS ROYAL SALUTE AT AKERSHUS FORTRESS

Yikes, Nilly thought.

Yeah, yeah, so what? Nilly thought.

Wait a minute, Nilly thought.

Maybe . . . Nilly thought.

He felt around in his back pocket. And there it was. He took it out. It was the half-chewed matchstick he'd got from Truls as payment for the bag of fartonaut powder. Of course it was wet and practically chewed in half, but it still had the red tip made of sulfur.

He held the matchstick in the beam of sunlight,

feeling how the sun warmed the skin on his hand. And two questions occurred to him. Number one: how long would you have to hold a match in the sun on a morning in mid-May before it was dry enough to light? And number two: how long does it take an anaconda to swim across the fjord from somewhere over by the Nesodden Peninsula?

You're going to get the answer right away. It takes *almost* exactly the same amount of time. Which is to say: it takes about one hour and four minutes to dry a match and for an anaconda to swim across the fjord from the Nesodden Peninsula and make its way deep into the Oslo sewer system, it only takes one hour and *three* minutes. So after an hour and three minutes had passed, Nilly had just noticed his hand starting to shake from holding it up in the beam of sunlight for so long, when he heard a familiar hissing noise.

Oh no, Nilly thought, since he felt that getting eaten once in twenty-four hours was more than enough.

He struck the match hard against the metal on the inside of the sewer pipe, but nothing happened.

The hissing noise came closer.

Nilly struck the match against the metal again. The red-tip sparked, but didn't light. And then Nilly was once again staring into the big pink mouth of the largest anaconda anyone had ever seen. The mouth came around the corner and Nilly thought, *This time that's it, a red-haired boy only gets so many chances.*

He pulled the match along the wall one last time.

It sparked. It sizzled. It ignited.

Nilly acted very quickly now. He set the match down in one of the holes left by the fangs in the crate with the burning end up. Then he dove into the water and swam away underwater as fast as he could. And for the first time he was glad that this was really nasty, filthy sewer water, where it would be impossible to see or smell much of anything besides nasty, filthy sewer water. And the match burned. From the top of the crate down into the highly explosive special gunpowder from Shanghai.

And for the second time that day, the foundations of downtown Oslo shook. On Sverdrup Street a manhole cover shot up into the air. Drivers slammed on their brakes and pedestrians froze on the pavement, staring at the hole in the street. The manhole cover was followed by a spray of wooden splinters and sewage. And then nothing. And then finally a tiny, red-haired and soaking wet boy climbed up out of the hole. He bowed politely to the frightened onlookers before rolling up his shirtsleeves.

Then he leaned over the manhole, spit some sewer water into it and yelled, "Take that, you earthworm!"

Before turning around to face the pedestrians, the shopkeepers who had come out of their shops to see what was going on and the drivers who had rolled down their windows.

"I'm Nilly!" the little boy yelled with his hands on his hips. "Anyone have anything to say about that?"

But the people on Sverdrup Street just stared, their mouths hanging open, at this strange being that had emerged from the inside of the earth.

"Nope, that's what I thought," said the boy, spitting one more time and walking away.

The Patent Office

WHEN THE BELL rang for first lesson Lisa was still wearing her band uniform. Everyone in the band was standing in the playground, talking about the weird thing that had happened that morning when they were marching through downtown Oslo. About the two band members who'd been knocked unconscious, about the ambulances that had come and about Conductor Madsen, who'd been so upset that they thought he might pass out as well.

Lisa pushed her way towards the classroom, through a crowd of children who were all pestering her and pulling on her and asking when they would be able to buy some fart powder because, after all, Independence Day was tomorrow!

Lisa was sitting at her desk when Mrs Strobe entered the classroom, pushed her glasses way out to the tip of her nose and peered at the one empty desk.

"Lisa, do you know if Mr Nilly is out sick today?"

Lisa just shook her head.

Mrs Strobe eyed her with suspicion. "Is something wrong, Lisa?"

Lisa really wanted to say no, but she knew that Mrs Strobe had a special kind of X-ray vision that could see through kids' skulls and into their brains, to where their thoughts were. So Lisa just came right out with it:

"Nilly's in jail."

A gasp ran through the classroom and Mrs Strobe raised one of her eyebrows so high that it totally vanished up into her hair.

"I'm sorry, could you please repeat that, Lisa?"

"Yes, Mrs Strobe. Nilly's in jail. Actually, to be specific, he's in the Dungeon of the Dead."

And then Mrs Strobe lowered both eyebrows and pulled them together so that it looked like she had a moustache on her forehead. "You used to be someone I could rely on to tell the truth, Lisa," she said. "But you've obviously been spending too much time with Mr Nilly."

"But I am telling the truth!" Lisa cried.

"Nonsense," Mrs Strobe scoffed. "Nilly is not in jail. Let's pick up reading where we left off. Page seventeen, everyone."

"He's in jail!" Lisa said.

"No!" said Mrs Strobe.

"Yes!" Lisa said.

"No," said a voice. "Not anymore."

Everyone in class turned around and looked at the door. And there was Nilly. He was soaking wet and the ends of his hair were a little singed, but otherwise he was exactly the same.

"Been swimming in the drinking fountain again, Mr Nilly?" Mrs Strobe asked sarcastically.

"Just a little altercation with a relatively large anaconda in the sewer, Mrs Strobe. And we handled it just fine with a couple of explosions."

The students all gasped, but were interrupted by Mrs Strobe slapping her desk with the palm of her hand.

"That's enough nonsense for today. Take your seat, Mr Nilly."

Nilly did as he was told, but as soon as he was seated he leaned over to Lisa. "I got your message," he whispered. "Sorry I wasn't able to get out sooner.

I was unfortunately delayed by a visit to the digestive system of a large snake. What's the situation?"

"Truls and Trym broke into Doctor Proctor's house last night," Lisa whispered. "And stole both jars of powder, as far as I could see."

"See? You just watched them do it?"

"Yup," Lisa said. "To make sure everything went according to plan."

"Plan? What plan?"

"Oh, just a teensy-weensy little emergency plan," Lisa said. "There's not really much to say."

AT THAT VERY moment five serious men were sitting behind a long table at the Oslo Patent Office. They were looking at Mr Trane, who was standing on the floor in front of them, going on and on about the amazing fartonaut powder that was in the jar he had set on the table in front of them.

"It's faster than a race car or a rocket," Mr Trane

said. "It's a better and cheaper fuel than a gazillion gallons of gasoline," he continued. "It can move men to the Moon, Mars and maybe Mercury."

As he talked and talked, the chairman – who was the most serious of the serious men – stared intently at Mr Trane. Because wasn't there something familiar, both about Mr Trane's name and his fat, pear-shaped body? Yes, he definitely reminded him of a boy in the neighbourhood he'd grown up in more than thirty years ago. A place called Hovseter. And this boy was always getting new pets since his old ones went crazy, kicked the bucket, or escaped. He vaguely remembered a Mongolian water vole. And a nice little snake from the Amazon. Could this be that same boy, all grown up?

When Mr Trane was done, the chairman cleared his throat and said, "All this is well and good, Mr Trane, but we here at the Oslo Patent Office cannot grant you a patent on what you call the . . . uh, fartonaut powder you say you invented if you don't know what it's made of. So, as the chairman of the Industrial Property Office, I am asking you for the third time. What is your invention made of?"

Mr Trane smiled as graciously as he could. "As I've already explained twice, I simply don't remember at all. It sort of happened by accident. I just tossed in a little of this, a little of that and stirred it up over a low heat. And then it turned into this powder that you see before you."

"Hmm," the chairman said seriously.

"Hmm," the four other serious men chimed in.

"We need proof," the chairman said.

"Yes, proof," the other four said.

"What kind of proof?" Mr Trane asked, looking at the clock. The men from NASA had said they'd be arriving on the two o'clock flight from Houston and he'd been hoping to have the patent signed and ready before he met with them at three.

"A test," the chairman said.

"Exactly!" the others said. "A patentable patent test."

Mr Trane looked at them uncertainly.

"You must demonstrate for us," the chairman said. "A very small dose, of course. Just so that we can see that what you're claiming appears reasonably likely."

"Of course," Mr Trane said, obviously nervous. "Of course, my dear gentlemen of the patent office."

"By all means, please wear that," said one of the serious men, pointing to a helmet hanging on a hook on the wall. "Although it didn't help the last man who used it very much."

"Who was that?" Mr Trane asked meekly.

"A man who thought he'd invented a new special gunpowder for the cannons at Akershus Fortress," the chairman said gravely. "It turned out it was far too explosive."

The other four shook their heads somberly and crossed themselves.

Then Mr Trane put on the helmet, walked up to the table and stuck the teaspoon down into the jar of powder, making sure he took only a tiny little bit. Then he swallowed, squeezed his eyes shut tight, and waited. And waited. And waited.

But nothing happened.

Nothing that he noticed, anyway.

But then he heard the five men starting to murmur back and forth to each other.

"Remarkable," one of them said.

"Highly unusual," the second one said.

"But haven't we seen this before?" the third one said.

Mr Trane cautiously opened one eye and saw the fourth man leafing through a big book.

"Here it is," the man said, pointing to the book. "This invention has already been patented."

The chairman cleared his throat and became even more serious. "Mr Trane, you are a fraud, who's trying to steal Doctor Proctor's invention."

Mr Trane stared and then sputtered, "Has that crazy professor already patented the fartonaut powder?"

"Fartonaut powder? Certainly not. We're talking about an essentially rather unsuccessful invention called Doctor Proctor's Light-Green Powder. Look for yourself, my dear sir!"

Mr Trane looked down at himself. And he emitted a shriek of disbelief. Because he was glowing a phosphorescent green and was partially transparent, like some kind of see-through larva.

AT THAT SAME instant, in Mrs Strobe's classroom, Nilly leaned over to Lisa's desk and whispered skeptically, "You did what?"

"I broke the cellar window, snuck in, and glued

a new label over the old one on the jar containing Doctor Proctor's Light-Green Powder."

"And on the new label you wrote . . . ?"

"Fartonaut Powder," Lisa giggled. "Keep Out of Reach of Children!"

They ducked as they saw Mrs Strobe's eyes sweeping across the classroom, searching for the source of the whispering.

"And then?" Nilly whispered.

"I put a jar full of regular fart powder next to the other jar. So Truls and Trym wouldn't suspect anything," she whispered. "Then I put all the fartonaut powder and the regular fart powder that were left in my backpack."

"And what did you do with all that powder?"

"Hid it in my wardrobe."

"And then you watched Truls and Trym . . . ?"

"Yup! I watched them from my bedroom window. They broke in and took both of the jars."

"I wonder where they are now. I didn't see them on the playground before the bell rang."

"Oh, I know where they are all right!" Lisa said, forgetting to whisper. "There was actually this very weird accident when the band was marching in downtown Oslo this morning. Something fell out of the sky – "

"Lisa!" Mrs Strobe slapped her desk. "Mr Nilly! What are you two talking about?"

Nilly cleared his throat. "We were just discussing why women like Lisa and yourself are so much smarter than men, Mrs Strobe," Nilly said. "I think women ought to take over the world."

Mrs Strobe looked at him, bewildered.

"But it was just a thought," Nilly said. "And since I'm a man, it was probably a very dumb thought. So I say let's forget the whole thing and thanks for your interest, Mrs Strobe. Please, just pick up where you left off."

The corners of Mrs Strobe's eyes twitched. Her prominent nose and the corners of her mouth twitched. But before she managed to say anything, there was a loud knock on the door.

"Come in!" she yelled quickly, actually sounding like she was relieved to have the interruption.

The door opened and there was a man standing there with a pair of dark sunglasses perched on a short, thick nose with black pores.

"Good day, Mrs Strobe," he said. "Pardon me for interrupting."

"Come in, Mr Madsen. What can we do for you?"

The director stepped into the classroom and cleared his throat. "We have a little crisis. Or to be more precise: a big crisis. As some of you know, there was a freak accident as our marching band was practising downtown this morning. Something very heavy and very hard and very unexpected fell out of the sky and hit two of our musicians on the head. They're in the hospital with mild concussions. The two students are Truls and Trym Trane."

A murmur spread through the classroom. And a couple of almost inaudible hurrahs could be heard. Mr Madsen cleared his throat again.

"And now the crisis is that the two of them will not be able to play with us in the Independence Day parade tomorrow. In other words, I'm looking for someone who can stand in for them at extremely short notice. Someone who plays the . . . uh, trumpet."

Lisa looked at Nilly, who was sitting there with his mouth hanging open, staring at Mr Madsen.

Mr Madsen shuffled his feet and looked like he was feeling sort of uncomfortable, but then he continued: "And if I'm not mistaken, there's someone in this class who plays the . . . uh, trumpet. A boy with . . . uh, perfect pitch. A boy named . . . uh, Nilly."

Everyone turned to look at the red-haired, tiny little guy who was now studying his nails with a distant, aloof expression.

"Nilly?" Mrs Strobe asked.

"Yes, Mrs Strobe?"

"Aren't you beside yourself with happiness, son? You're going to get to play with Mr Madsen in the Dølgen School Marching Band in the big parade on the seventeenth of May!"

Nilly squeezed one eye shut and stared thoughtfully off into space. "The seventeenth of May, May seventeenth, that date sounds familiar . . . oh, yeah, now I remember! Isn't that Norwegian Independence Day? Because first of all I already have a lot of plans for Independence Day. I was planning to drink some traditional eggnog. Then there are a few sack races I'm signed up for. And then of course I have to defend my title as the reigning champion of the Great Egg-Rolling Race in Eggedal. And that's even in the toughest group, the hard-boiled egg group."

The kids started laughing, but an extraordinarily powerful palm-against-teacher's-desk slap shut them all up again immediately. Apart from Nilly, of course.

"In short," he said. "It may be difficult for me to squeeze any trumpet playing in on that particular day."

Mr Madsen grimaced and groaned in despair.

"Unless . . . ," Nilly said.

"Yes?" Mr Madsen lit up. "Yes, tell me!"

"Unless I'm asked very nicely, of course . . ."

"Yes, yes, I'm asking nicely!" Mr Madsen cried out.

"Or even better, unless I'm begged."

"I'm begging, I'm begging!" Mr Madsen wailed.

"On your knees?" Nilly asked.

And Mr Madsen dropped to his knees and begged while Mrs Strobe's glasses slid twenty inches down her nose at this unusual sight.

"All right!" Nilly said, leaping up onto his desk. "I'll play. Just make sure you have a uniform that's small enough."

And then all the kids cheered. So did Mr Madsen. And although it was hard to tell, even Mrs Strobe did, a little bit, on the inside. And while they were cheering, Lisa whispered a few words into Nilly's ear. And then he stuck two fingers into his mouth and whistled so loudly that the keyhole in the door made a squeaking sound and suddenly it got totally quiet again.

"Now, a message for all children!" Nilly yelled. "This afternoon we'll be selling fart powder in Lisa's garden. Right, Lisa?"

"Yeah," Lisa said, jumping up on her desk. "And we're lowering the price to two kroner, since . . . well, since it's cheaper."

"Isn't she smart?" Nilly smiled.

And with that the cheering started again and since

the bell rang right then, Lisa and Nilly were carried out of the room in triumph.

Mrs Strobe and Mr Madsen were left standing there in the classroom watching them go, shaking their heads and laughing.

"Those two are quite a pair, aren't they?" Mr Madsen said.

"They sure are," Mrs Strobe said. "But there was just one thing I was wondering about."

"Yeah?"

"What hit Truls and Trym?"

"That's the most mysterious part of the whole thing," Mr Madsen said. "Believe it or not, it was a manhole cover."

The Confession

EVENING HAD FALLEN and in just one night
it would be the seventeenth of May, Norwegian
Independence Day, when all children and grown-ups
put on their traditional costumes and march in parades
until they get blisters and their feet swell up so much
they can't get their brand-new shoes off. They yell

"Hurrah" until their voices are so hoarse they wouldn't even be able to whine when they stuff themselves way too full of hot dogs and ice cream and their stomachs feel like they are crammed full of barbed wire. In other words, it was the evening before the day that all children and grown-ups were really looking forward to.

And on this evening Truls woke up and discovered that he was lying in a hospital bed. He looked around and discovered Trym lying awake in the bed next to him.

"What happened?" Truls asked. "Why do you have a bandage around your head?"

"A manhole cover," Trym said. "And you have a bandage around your head too."

"We were supposed to sell fart powder to the kids and make a fortune today!" Truls said. "Independence Day is tomorrow!"

"And we were supposed to play the trumpet," Trym said, dazed.

Right then the door to the room opened and a nurse came in.

"Hi, boys," she said. "There are two people here to see you."

"Daddy!" Truls yelled, on the verge of tears, he was so relieved.

"And Mummy!" Trym whimpered.

"Not quite," the nurse said, stepping to the side.

Truls and Trym stiffened in their beds. Before

them stood two men that we have met before. They were wearing their police uniforms and tucked under their arms each of them was holding a jar that we've also seen before.

"Good evening, boys," Mr Fu Manchu said. "I trust your head injuries won't be permanent."

"And," Mr Handlebar added, "that you'll be able to confess right away that you were the ones who broke into Doctor Proctor's cellar."

"And stole these jars," Mr Handlebar continued.

"It wasn't me," Truls blurted.

"Or me," whimpered Trym.

"We followed a tip and found them in your garage," Mr Handlebar said.

"And we also found two pairs of shoes there with glass shards in the soles. Like the glass shards that came from the broken glass in the cellar. You're done for."

"But if you'll give us a confession now, you may

be able to avoid winding up in the Dungeon of the Dead."

"It was me," Truls blurted.

"No, it was me," Trym whimpered.

"And Dad," Truls said.

"Yes, Dad," Trym said. "He . . . he . . . tricked us."

"We were duped." Truls sniffed.

"We're so easily tricked," Trym sobbed. "Poor us!"

"Hmm," Mr Fu Manchu said. "Mr Trane, you say. Just as we thought. We should put out an A.P.B."

"Yeah," Mr Handlebar said. "And fast. Neither he nor that dreadful Hummer of his were home when we checked."

Mr Fu Manchu got out his police radio and called the police station. "Put out an A.P.B. for all cars to stop any black Hummers they see. We're looking for a man named Mr Trane. He's incredibly dangerous. I repeat: incredibly dangerous."

And with that he started the biggest car chase in

Oslo's history. We won't go into details, but more than one hundred police cars chased Mr Trane's black Hummer as it raced through the streets of Oslo, spewing out more carbon dioxide than two locomotives. Every time the police blocked off a street and thought they had him, Mr Trane just gave the Hummer more gas and broke through the barricades, speeding past the police cars, the police horses and the policemen all over downtown Oslo.

And that's what they were still doing when the sun rose and Independence Day was finally here.

Independence Day

FOR THE LAST time in this story the sun rose in a cloudless sky. It had already shone for a while on Japan, Russia and Sweden, and now it was starting to shine on the very small capital city, of a very small country called Norway. The sun got right to work shining on the yellow, and fairly small, palace that was home to the king of Norway, who didn't rule over enough for it to amount to anything, but who was looking forward to waving at the children's parade as it marched by and to listening to the Big and Almost World-Famous Royal Salute in his honour. And of course the sun shone on Akershus Fortress, on the old cannons that were aimed out over the Oslo Fjord and onto the most remote of doors. The door that ultimately led to the city's most feared jail cell, the Dungeon of the Dead.

And just at this moment the door to the Dungeon of the Dead opened and out onto the grassy embankment stepped Doctor Proctor, who had to squint in the sunlight. He was followed by two guards.

"Hip hip hurrah!" yelled Nilly and Lisa, who were standing there waiting for him. They jumped up and down and waved their Norwegian flags.

"Freedom, sunshine, Independence Day and my assistants," Doctor Proctor said, laughing and hugging them. "Could the day get any better?"

"For some," mumbled the Commandant, who was standing a few steps behind Lisa and Nilly and rocking back and forth on his heels.

"But nobody's told me why I was set free," the doctor said after he set Nilly and Lisa down.

"Truls and Trym admitted everything," Lisa said. "That they bullied Nilly into giving them the fartonaut powder that day."

"And that you never sold fartonaut powder to children," Nilly said.

"And the police are going to have Mr Trane in custody soon," Lisa said. "For stealing the powder and passing it off as his own. They just have to finish racing around the city first."

"Good heavens!" the professor said. "Then all of the problems are solved!"

"Not quite all," Lisa said, nodding towards the Commandant. "Dad?"

"Of course, of course," rumbled the Commandant, stepping forwards. He seemed embarrassed; maybe that was why he spoke a little louder and more commandingly than necessary. "Yes, well, we are so sorry for this idiotic imprisonment, Doctor Proctor. It won't happen again. Unless you do something very illegal, of course. Like stuffing bananas in exhaust pipes, for example. Or hoisting infants up to the tops of flagpoles. Or . . ."

"Get to the point, Dad," Lisa said sternly.

"Of course, of course, the point," rumbled the Commandant, his neck reddening a little. "As you can see, we have some old cannons over there. And as you can't see, we don't have any special gunpowder from Shanghai, which we need for the Big and Almost World-Famous Royal Salute that was supposed to be fired off from these cannons later today. It has never happened before in the modern era that the Royal Salute hasn't been fired off, and we're afraid the whole world will laugh at us. Well, all of northern Europe, anyway . . . except maybe Finland . . . and . . . and . . ."

"Dad!"

"Of course, of course. The question is — "

"The question is," Doctor Proctor interrupted, "whether I can help you with the Royal Salute. And the answer, my dear Commandant and neighbour, is: *yes!*"

And with that, cheering broke out for the second time in a very short period. But Lisa and Nilly weren't able to cheer for very long, because of course they were about to go perform in the Dølgen School Marching Band in the Independence Day parade.

THE DØLGEN SCHOOL Marching Band marched and played like never before. They hit a lot of the right notes and had never been closer to playing in time. And Nikolai Amadeus Madsen led the way in his sunglasses and grinned his biggest smile as he dreamed of the marching band competition at Eidsvoll that summer.

Lisa played the clarinet and every once in a while she glanced over at Nilly, who practically had to do splits to keep up with everyone else. But he played amazingly well as his fingers danced over the keys, his eyes hurriedly scanning the music.

The band had reached Sverdrup Street and Nilly was concentrating so hard that he didn't hear the wailing sirens of the police cars approaching. And he didn't see the big, roaring Hummer turn the corner on squealing tyres and slam on its brakes when it saw that its path was finally blocked by something it couldn't just run over or push out of the way: a whole Independence Day parade marching towards it. And the noise the school marching band was making sent shivers down the driver's spine, because it was the sound of an explosion, a plane crash and an avalanche all at the same time.

Following the Hummer roughly a hundred police cars turned the corner with their blue lights and sirens.

A man jumped out of the Hummer.

Lisa stopped playing. "But isn't that . . ." she said. "It is! It's Mr Trane."

Nilly stopped playing too and looked up.

Mr Trane was standing in the middle of the street, looking around frantically. There was nowhere to hide. It seemed like this was the end of the chase.

"Ha!" Mr Trane yelled. "You'll never get me, you idiots, you worthless turds!" And with that he yanked up the manhole cover next to him and jumped down into the hole.

"Hey!" Lisa said.

The policemen ran over, peered down into the hole, scratched their heads and discussed the situation. Nilly and Lisa could make out a few random snippets of the conversation:

"I'm wearing my Independence Day uniform today, and I don't want to go down in the sewer and get it all dirty."

"Well I have asthma; the smell of excrement just isn't good for me."

"And I'm signed up for a sack race."

So they shoved the manhole cover back into place, checked to make sure it was on tight, cancelled the whole police chase and waved the Independence Day parade on.

ANNA CONDA WAS lying in the pipe, listening to its stomach rumble with hunger. It could hear the noise of a marching band and smell the scent of boiled hot dogs from up on the street. And now, suddenly, it heard a huge splash in the Oslo sewer system. The creature was so hungry that it was only just barely able to swim towards the sound. But when it got there, it saw something it recognised. Two-legged food glowing a faint green. The last time it had eaten something like this, Anna Conda had been blasted all the way out to the Nesodden Peninsula. But that wasn't the only thing it recognised. There was something about this two-legged food, something familiar from when the creature was a little anaconda snakeling in a cage in Hovseter. Because wasn't there a certain similarity between this fat, fleshy, sausagelike man and that fat boy who used to poke sticks in his side back then? Yes, that was it! And now the anaconda could see that the man had noticed it and that the recognition was mutual. And that the man had opened his mouth to scream. That his mouth was as far open as it would go. Which was very far. But of course nowhere near as far open as Anna Conda's mouth now was.

"WOW, THAT WAS good!" Nilly yelled as he chewed. He was holding a steaming hot dog in a bun.

"Really good!" Lisa said, taking a bite of her hot dog.

They were sitting on the grassy embankment at Akershus Fortress, watching the seven brave guardsmen who were pacing nervously in front of the table where Doctor Proctor was standing with a big jar of Doctor Proctor's Totally Normal Fart Powder. The seven of them had signed up as volunteers for this honourable assignment.

"Assistant Nilly!" Doctor Proctor yelled, glancing up at the clock on the tower at City Hall, which was approaching the time of the Big and Almost World-Famous Royal Salute. "Can you help me dole out the portions?"

"Of course," Nilly said and scarfed down the rest of his hot dog, ran over to the table, grabbed the wooden ladle that was lying there and stuck it down into the jar.

"I'm Nilly," he told the guardsmen. "What do you have to say about that?"

One of the guardsmen started swaying back and forth and singing "Silly Nilly." Two more quickly joined in.

"Shut up," Nilly said, looking at the clock. "Or rather, open up. And bend over. Quick, we only have seconds to go."

"Is it dangerous?" one of the guardsmen asked nervously, opening his mouth.

"Yes," Nilly said and stuck a whole ladleful of powder into the guardman's mouth. "But it tastes like pears. Nine . . . eight . . ."

"Thanks, assistant," the professor said, adjusting his motorcycle goggles. "My dear guardsmen, please assume your positions."

The guardsmen, who were not used to following commands that included words like "dear" and "please," looked at each other in confusion.

"I feel a little tickle in my stomach," one of them said.

"Listen up!!" the small, red-haired boy bellowed. "Point your rear ends in the same directions as the cannons, now! And bend over!"

This was a language the guardsmen understood and they followed the orders immediately.

And right then the clock on the Town Hall tower started to toll twelve times.

IT WAS SUCH a funny sight that Lisa had to laugh out loud. Seven guards bending over with their rear ends aimed out over the wall of the fortress at the Oslo Fjord as the Town Hall clock chimed.

But after the third chime neither Lisa nor any of the other inhabitants of Oslo and the surrounding area heard the clock anymore. Because both it and Lisa's laughter were drowned out by a bang so loud that frost formed on people's eardrums and their eyes were pressed quite a way back into their heads. The next bang sent a rush of air up Rosenkrantz Street to Karl Johan Street, where it made all the flags stand out straight. The third bang shattered three window-panes on the Nesodden Peninsula and made the grand, old apple trees in the Ullevål Garden town burst into bloom out of sheer fright. The fourth bang caused a girl Lisa knew in Sarpsborg to look up at the cloud-less sky and wonder if a thunderstorm was approaching. The fifth wasn't that loud at all; it just sounded like a fart and made the people in Oslo look at each other in surprise. But the sixth nearly caused a cruise ship in the middle of the fjord on its way to Denmark to capsize and a flight of swallows on their way to Norway changed their minds and decided to fly back to Africa. The sound wave reached all the way to Trafalgar Square in London, where it bent the spray from the fountain so that all the tourists standing

around it got wet and children laughed with glee.

When the final and seventh bang rang out, the king in his castle nodded in satisfaction at the farting and thought he had never heard a finer salute. And before the last echo had faded into silence, the king's adjutant was already on the phone to the Commandant of Akershus Fortress to tell him that the king would like to award him and his cannoneers the Royal Medal of Merit, a promotion to honourary cannoneer and a long and happy life.

"Can he really give us a long life?" the Commandant asked skeptically.

"He's the king," the adjutant said, hanging up the phone, offended.

The Commandant walked out onto the embankment again, where seven guardsmen with rips in the seats of their trousers, two policemen with their eyes wet from tears of laughter and Lisa, Nilly and the professor were still dancing around in joy.

The Last Chapter

IT HAD BEEN a looooong Independence Day and there was still a little of it left.

The afternoon sun shone lazily on the pear tree in Doctor Proctor's garden, and Lisa and Nilly sat underneath it, each in their own chair, clutching their stomachs. Along with the professor, they'd polished off a three-metre-long jelly, and now they were so full that the professor had gone inside to rest a little.

"You did great today," Lisa said.

"You didn't do so badly yourself," Nilly admitted. "It was all thanks to you."

"You think?" Lisa smiled, closing her eyes to the rays of sunlight that filtered through the leaves.

"Yeah," Nilly said. "You're the smartest girl I know. And even more important, you're the best . . ."

It got quiet and Lisa opened her eyes and was surprised to see that Nilly's face had become really red. And she thought he might have got something stuck in his throat because he had to clear it three times before he was able to continue in a slightly hoarse voice.

"You're the best friend anyone could have."

"Thanks," Lisa said, her whole body feeling warm. "So are you."

And then neither of them knew what to say, so maybe it was just as well that there was a *bang*. Because there was. There was a final bang on this loooooong Independence Day and they both turned towards Doctor Proctor's cellar. Because this didn't sound like Doctor Proctor's Totally Normal Fart Powder.

"Oh, no," Lisa said, dismayed.

"Not the fartonaut powder . . ." Nilly said.

"No," said Doctor Proctor, appearing in the cellar doorway. His face was black with soot and oil. "Just a faulty muffler on a motorcycle that hasn't been started in twelve years. But that just needed a little lubrication to run, well, like it had been lubricated."

And with that the professor drove his motorcycle and sidecar out of the cellar and through the high grass, stopping in front of them. There was a brown, worn leather suitcase in the sidecar.

Nilly and Lisa stood up.

"Where are you going?" Nilly asked.

"Where do you think, my fartonaut assistant?" the professor asked, beaming under his hockey helmet and motorcycle goggles.

"You're going to Paris," Lisa said. "You're going to try to find Juliette Margarine."

"Wish me luck," Doctor Proctor said. "And lock the cellar and keep an eye on my house until I get back."

"Good luck," Nilly said.

They walked ahead of the motorcycle and opened the gate.

The professor revved the engine and it gave a satisfying growl.

"And if you go through Sarpsborg . . ." Lisa said.

"Yes?"

"Then you can say hello to my *second* best friend."

And the last rays of sunlight shone on the pear tree, on Nilly's red hair, on Lisa's smile and maybe on a tiny tear, as Doctor Proctor's motorcycle and sidecar drove away down Cannon Avenue.